DEAD MAN'S TRENCH

NORFOLK COZY MYSTERIES

KEITH FINNEY

Keith Finney - Author

DEAD MAN'S TRENCH

NORFOLK COZY MYSTERIES

KEITH FINNEY

AN INVITATION

Welcome to your invitation to join my Readers' Club.

Receive free, exclusive content only available to members including short stories, character interviews and much more.

To join, look out for the link towards the end of this book and you're in!

1

IN A HOLE

Alan Fairchild's blood pressure wasn't in a good place.

Getting the head of archaeology at Cambridge University to meet Stanton Parva's history group was a coup.

Why on earth turn out if they won't listen? Alan fumed in his thoughts. Did no one care that he'd sweat blood to secure a private tour of the dig, which he knew to be of national importance?

"May I emphasise again," said Professor Pullman, as heads swivelled and old friends chatted. "On no account interfere with the excavations you will see this morning."

It was an unequal battle. The gentle waters of Stanton Broad, glistening in the morning sun, had much more appeal than a dusty academic. Add in a golden carpet of Norfolk reed swaying rhythmically in the breeze, and the result was inevitable.

"Our hypothesis is that this vast Roman villa complex was wantonly destroyed. All the signs point to Boudica, queen of the Iceni Tribe. In around AD 60 she led a revolt against the Roman legions. Also..."

The professor's words failed to impress one section of

the group as they soaked up the latest village gossip. First amongst equals was Phyllis Abbott, a sprite eighty-two-year-old whose loss of hearing caused her to shout then accuse others of not speaking the queen's English.

Alan tried a flanking manoeuvre to work his way around the rebels so he could get close to Phyllis, who was in deep discussion with her best friend, Betty.

Phyllis was lamenting the post office's move from the village shop, which she'd run until age seventy-one, to the petrol station on the outskirts of Stanton Parva.

"Modernising the post office is what they call it. How come making things worse can be better for the customer? And what Her Majesty must think about it, well, I just don't know. What do you think, Betty?"

Betty nodded as she attempted a reply.

"Well, yes... I suppose..."

Phyllis was having none of it.

"There's no supposing about it. How do I get to Flatley's petrol station with my leg? Then there's the price of a first-class stamp. Shocking, that's what I say."

By now, Alan had sidled up to the pair and knew from Betty's scowl that she'd given up any hope of challenging her friend's views on the subject.

"Shush," said Alan, a wobble in his voice letting slip that his nerves were getting the better of him.

Phyllis shot Alan a cold stare.

"Who are you shushing, young man? Just like your mother, you are."

The old woman dismissed Alan with an imperious wave of her hand before turning back to Betty.

"And you know what?"

"No. What, dear?" offered Betty, pleased to be asked her opinion.

"When I went to pay for my Jiffy bag, that stupid boy asked which pump I was using. Well, I thought he was talking about the thing Dr Bridlington prescribed me. I told him to mind his own business. Then..."

The rest of the group were torn between Boudica chasing out the Romans and Phyllis' medicinal pump.

Alan had had enough.

"Er, excuse me, Phyllis, but I'm sixty-five, and my mother's been dead for fifteen years."

Half turning, she switched conversation from Betty to Alan without missing a beat.

"I remember you when you were in shorts. They called you snot sleeve, didn't they? And your mother still owes me for a pint of milk," said Phyllis, before once more engaging Betty in the thorny issue of Jiffy bags.

Alan withdrew, trying hard to act as if his run-in with Phyllis hadn't happened.

Keen to regain a measure of control, he turned to the professor.

"May I ask if the villa's location had anything to do with the expanse of open water?"

It was a question to which he already knew the answer, but anything was better than another rebuke from Phyllis.

"Ah," replied the professor, pleased once more to be the centre of attention. "In fact, the Broads weren't dug until the twelfth century when the growing population needed peat for cooking and heating."

Alan's relief was palpable as the academic gave a positive response to his question.

Professor Pullman waxed lyrical about the abandoned peat diggings being filled over time by rising water levels to form the Broads, until the manic laughter of a Minions mobile ringtone interrupted his flow.

Alan strained to see where the sound was coming from and meandered through the group until he came across Angela Simms, who was rummaging through her enormous shoulder bag to silence the din.

"Can you manage?" asked Alan, sensing Angela's embarrassment.

"Never you mind this lot. They can tut all they like."

Alan shook his head in admonishment at two male members of the group.

"You can moan all you like, but just think, what if someone was trying to get an urgent message to you? Until you take the call, you don't know why they're ringing, do you?"

The two men half turned from Alan, shrugging their shoulders like two naughty schoolboys.

Alan turned back towards Angela just in time to see her retrieve the mobile and scurry from the group, her face etched with concern.

As Professor Pullman seized his opportunity to round off his introduction to the site, he turned from the group, lifted his right arm, and urged the assembly to follow as he set a blistering pace towards a small mound in the middle distance.

It took a couple of minutes for Alan to realise Angela hadn't rejoined the group. Fearful she had received bad news, he scanned the field to see where she might be.

A hundred yards or so to his left he noticed the young woman standing ramrod straight, frozen to the spot.

Alan quietly backed away from the group and ambled towards the woman, not wanting to draw attention to himself—or to Angela.

As he neared, he noticed Angela held both arms to her sides. Her phone hung limply in one hand.

Oh Lord, he thought.

"Is everything okay, Ang?" said Alan in a low, quiet tone, keen not to startle her.

She didn't respond.

Alan slipped the mobile from her hand and raised it to his ear. Angela offered no resistance. He turned and walked a few paces back towards the distant group.

"Ang, are you still there? How's the signal? Can you hear me?"

Alan spoke into the handset, trying his best not to alarm the caller.

"Hi, she's fine but tied up for a minute or two. I'll get her to give you a ring back. Is that okay?"

Alan didn't wait for a response. Instead, he ended the call, switched the mobile to silent, and slipped it into his shirt pocket.

Retracing his steps towards Angela, both now stood at the edge of a deep excavation.

Alan saw what she saw.

The body of a man.

2

THE WALLED GARDEN

The eyes were open, face drained of colour. A trickle of congealed blood puddled in the dusty ground to the side of his head.

"I knew that bugger would come to a sticky end one day"

Alan, startled at the sudden sound of voices, turned to see Phyllis at the head of a small group of club members, who had wandered over, curious at Alan's earlier departure.

The old woman showed no sign of shock. It wasn't the first time Phyllis had observed violent death. War service had seen to that.

Alan instinctively moved closer to Angela, who hadn't moved a muscle.

He looked across to Phyllis admiring her composure but puzzled by her comment.

"What do you mean?"

"Well, they don't... or should I say, didn't, call Fred Collins 'Narky' for nothing. He was a bad-tempered bully, that one."

"Mrs Abbott," Alan responded, not sure how to finish

the sentence. Simultaneously, he turned Angela away from the horror. She offered no resistance.

"It's true," Phyllis continued, her voice quiet now yet still lacking any trace of sympathy for the dead man. "He always picked on the young 'uns from the 'big house.' He knew they couldn't answer back."

Alan returned to the edge of the excavation. He shook his head.

"What a waste."

Phyllis fumed. "Waste? What do you mean? He thought he was God's gift to women. Always trying to paw them. I've seen him do it. Given him a piece of my mind more than once, I have."

Phyllis kicked some loose earth into the trench, watching it settle like unwanted confetti on the dead man's exposed cheek and shoulder.

Alan recoiled, at last summoning the courage to challenge the old woman.

"For the love of God, Phyllis. Show some humanity, will you? No one deserves to die like *that*."

The old woman tilted her head upward and sniffed the air, dismissing his show of sympathy for the dead man.

She pointed a spindly finger towards the corpse.

"Seen this in the war. Men who lord it over other lads. Try it on with their girlfriends. When a jealous man gets his blood up, he can do anything. And from what I know, plenty had it in for that fat sod."

Before Alan could respond, he noticed the remainder of the group approaching and headed them off before they reached the excavation.

"There's been a terrible accident," said Alan. "We need to call the police. I'll try and get through on my mobile, but to make sure we do, I need someone to run over to the big house and raise the alarm."

All eyes descended on Sid. He was the youngest by decades.

"I ll do it," replied Sid, making off at a sprint towards Stanton Hall.

ENJOYING the solitude of the Hall's walled garden, Anthony Stanton filled his lungs with a riot of heady scents. As the dew lifted into Norfolk's big sky, the effect seemed all the stronger.

This place is about as far from work as I can get, he thought.

Anthony kicked a spray of gravel from the pathway, cutting its way through blazing beds of late-summer flowers.

He flopped onto a rickety, cast-iron bench and tilted his head backwards. A warming sun had the desired effect.

For the first time in a long time, he pushed painful memories to the back of his mind.

The quiet didn't last long. Reacting in an instant to the sharp crack of a rusty gate latch lifting, he hunched over as if to make himself as small as possible, his attention focused on a dark outline filling the gate opening.

Anthony squinted at the silhouetted figure of a woman.

"Excuse me, this area is private."

The voice was assertive. He expected compliance.

Ignoring his words, the woman continued to close the distance between them.

"So it's true. You're back, Anthony... and in one piece too. Lucky for you they couldn't shoot straight."

He recognised the voice. Using the long form of his first name was a giveaway. She always did that to provoke him.

He chose not to react.

"Military training has its uses."

"Hello, you," said Lyn.

"Hello, you," he replied.

The ease of their exchanges had all the familiarity of a long-married couple relaxed in each other's company.

"Still breaking the rules, Lyn. Just like at school... and the Hall still isn't open to the public today."

Lyn smiled, unmoved by his halfhearted rebuke.

"Just as well I'm not Joe Public, then, isn't it? And as for school, we couldn't all be the class swot, could we?"

Lyn's barbed comment rolled back the years to a time when they were at Stanton Primary together.

He gave a throaty laugh. Time had passed, but the constant ribbing he got from his classmates had stayed with him. He'd always seemed to come top in exams, but it wasn't the only reason he stuck out. Ant spoke differently and lived in "the big house."

His smile widened as he recalled how she was the one who controlled the others. A talent, he suspected, Lyn still possessed, judging by the confidence in her voice and the way she held herself.

"Wasn't my fault my parents bought in to that swinging-sixties hippie thing, and sent me to the local primary school for oiks instead of public school."

Lyn gave him a sideways look and shook her head in that dismissive way only she could get away with.

"Playing the victim doesn't suite you, Ant, and anyway, you wouldn't have suited pinstriped trousers or a straw boater. At least your parents spoke to each other in words with more than one syllable and lived in the same place."

"Things any better now?" Ant responded.

Lyn let out an almost inaudible sigh.

"Let's put it this way, at least Mum has stopped throwing things at Dad. Mind you, living at opposite ends of the village helps."

Ant didn't pursue the point and broke eye contact knowing the damage went deeper than Lyn would ever admit.

"Anyway, I popped over to drop off a chocolate cake to your parents. It's their favourite, you know. I bring one over every Saturday."

Ant smiled as Lyn flopped next to him on the bench.

"I didn't think you'd come back after Greg's death."

Ant rolled his head as if to make sure his exposed skin captured every ray the sun had to offer. His arms hung across the back rail of the bench. Lyn didn't try to avoid contact as she settled back.

"I didn't intend to stay away for so long. At eighteen you think your parents will live forever. I'm still not sure if I'm back for good, even though..."

Ant faltered. He shuffled his feet in the gravel.

Lyn stared into the distance, looking at nothing in particular.

"A flying visit, then? Your brother's been dead a long time, and the estate seems to run itself from what I can see."

Ant gave a short, sharp laugh.

"That's just the problem, Lyn. You know better than me how frail Mum and Dad are. To tell you the truth, it was a shock."

He stopped, sensing Lyn's reaction.

Another telling-off coming.

"For heaven's sake, Ant. They're both in their eighties, and the man had a heart attack a few months ago. What did you expect?"

Ant shrugged his shoulders and changed tack. It was

easier than thinking about his parents not being around forever.

"The thing is, Lyn, the estate's in a right mess, and I'm not cut out to fix it."

Lyn sensed his unease.

"That was Greg's job. And what happens? He flips his car into Stanton Broad, and goodnight Vienna."

"Sounds like you're feeling sorry for yourself again, Anthony."

There she goes again.

"Not at all," replied Ant. "I'm just stating a fact. It was Greg's inheritance, not mine. Turns out the estate income has been slipping for years, and the Hall is in a hell of a state. You've seen the water damage. Dad's tried, but it's too much. To make things worse, people paid to look after the place just haven't done their jobs."

Lyn's expression softened.

Ant settled back into the bench, his head once more falling backwards as the sun bathed his face.

"Isn't it strange, Lyn. You know, when you're a kid, you look up to your parents and assume they know it all. Then whether it's poor health or just getting older, you realise they're not invincible after all. You must see it all the time."

Ant opened an eye and squinted into a bright Norfolk sky.

"Dad mentioned you started as head teacher at our old school in September. Spooky or what!"

He let out a throaty laugh.

"Come to think of it, it's kind of strange dealing with stuff in classrooms I sat in as a child," replied Lyn. "But you're right. I see kids affected by things at home. There's a familiar look in their eyes when voices are raised—*a rabbit caught in the headlights* type of look. Despite working like stink, sometimes we can't fix things. But we try. That's all anyone can do."

Ant sensed her sudden nervousness and could have kicked himself for making her remember her own childhood traumas.

"Sorry, Lyn. Didn't mean to do that, I know you had it tough at home."

After a few moments of uneasy silence, Lyn gave Ant a sideways glance as she playfully pinched the skin of his arm between two fingers.

Ant winced in mock pain but made no move to distance himself from the attack.

"That's something else you did in class, remember?" said Ant. "I never understood why."

Lyn smiled.

"Let's just say it was my way of toughening you up," she replied.

Ant had to admit Lyn had got him out of several sticky situations with Jezza, the class bully.

"Of course, there's another explanation."

Lyn gave Ant a puzzled look. She was at risk of overacting.

"And that would be?"

"Affection, Lyn. I asked my father once why you kept hitting me when you spent most of your time fending off Hillier and his thugs. Dad was clear about it, and seeing as I didn't have a better explanation, I believed him!"

Lyn waved at Ant dismissively.

"In your dreams, Anthony Stanton. My older brother used to pinch me, so I took it out on you. One snotty boy was just the same as any other to me. Anyhow, you sat next to me and were daft enough not to fight back."

Both laughed, the interlude having served as a convenient pressure valve for less-happy memories.

"Right. Time for a piece of chocolate cake and a cup of tea with your parents."

As she spoke, Lyn sprang from the rickety bench and launched herself towards the gate.

"Haven't I endured enough pain for one day without being exposed to your baking?" moaned Ant as he sprinted to make up the distance between them.

"Remember that nut caramel toffee you made with salted peanuts in year four? Yuck!"

Without stopping, Lyn bent down, scooped a handful of gravel and tossed it over her head.

"And before you say anything, if I'd have wanted to hit you, I would have. You're not the only one who's a crack shot."

The levity didn't last long. As Lyn reached out to lift the latch of the gate it moved towards her at speed, causing Lyn to cry out in pain as the heavy construction smacked into her.

"Oh, er... sorry, miss. Only..."

Ant's instinct was to shout at the lad. The look of panic on the youth's face stopped him from doing so.

The boy didn't wait for either a welcome or reprimand.

"It's your land agent, sir. He's, er... sort of... dead."

Ant felt a swell of frustration at the youth's nervous ramblings.

"What do you mean, 'sort of'? Either someone is dead, or they are not dead."

Ant glimpsed Lyn's look of disapproval and knew he'd gone too far.

Sid looked no less frustrated as he tried to make himself understood.

"Up at the dig site. He's in a ditch. They told me to fetch the police."

Ant pointed towards the elegant columns fronting the imposing entrance to the Hall.

"The phone's in the hallway. And you'd better ask for an ambulance."

3

OIL ON TROUBLED WATERS

Lyn dismounted Ant's quad bike with care, relieved to have arrived at the dig site in one piece.

"Please, Ladies and Gentlemen," Alan pleaded, "come away from the trench. The police will be here soon. They will not think well of you tramping all over a possible crime scene."

Ant knew Alan had a point. The force's first action would be to secure the scene and protect possible evidence.

Lyn watched as Ant's bearing changed from chillaxed companion to military commander. She winced inwardly as he barked a command.

"We've a few minutes before they arrive, so let's get organised."

Lyn moved into head-teacher mode striking the perfect balance between assertiveness and mother hen.

"Come along, you lot. Let's get you over here to gather your thoughts. I expect the police will wish to take statements from you all."

A quick glance at Ant told Lyn she had his approval.

"Over here" amounted to a pile of soil about fifty feet from the trench.

The prospect of being interviewed by the police did the trick in getting the group's attention.

"Murdered by a jealous husband," said Phyllis.

"I think it was Jed. He was always arguing with Narky," offered Betty.

"Nonsense. He was a drunk, and I reckon he tripped and fell—stupid man," chipped in Graham Drake, known by all not to have been a fan of the deceased.

"You never liked him, did you?" shouted Simon Green from the edge of the group. "Be careful what you say when the bobbies arrive, or they'll have you."

Graham Drake looked less than impressed with Simon, but then he'd never got on with him either.

Lyn had had enough.

"You'd all better be careful what you say to the police. It's not a murder mystery weekend you're on, you know. Whatever you say, the police will check."

Lyn's mild rebuke did the trick as she watched several heads drop a little with eyes fixed on the ground like naughty schoolchildren. Except Phyllis.

"Are you suggesting we keep quiet when the cops come?"

Lyn chose not to rise to the elderly woman's bait.

"I'm suggesting you tell them what you know and what you saw, not what you would have liked to have heard or seen... and Phyllis... cops? Really?"

"For God's sake, young man. Can't you do anything right?"

'Professor. It slipped. Anyway, it was only a..."

Ant watched the academic explode with anger.

"It was only what? Are you trying to tell me what is, and what is not, historically important on my dig?"

Simon Hangmead froze as he surveyed the shattered fragments of a Roman oil lamp, which formed a neat arc around his feet.

"What's the matter?" asked Ant as he looked up from the bottom of the trench to see the professor launching into a terrified-looking, young man.

Shaking his head in frustration, the professor broke off eye contact with his student, turned towards the voice, and bent forward to peer over the excavation.

"Lord Stanton, I..."

"That's me. Now, what can I do for you?"

The professor looked troubled, though not about the dead man.

"My excavation. Please, may I ask you to refrain from—"

Ant cut off the professor.

"Which is on my father's land, Professor." Ant worked hard to stifle his emotions.

Did this stupid man not care a man lay dead, possibly murdered?

Ant could tell from the professor's irritated look that he was unused to being interrupted.

"As you say, er, your family's land."

The academic's apparent submissiveness failed to impress Ant whose steely eyes made plain who was in control.

"You see, the university insist I bring a certain number of undergraduates on each dig, irrespective of ability. All in the cause of widening participation, whatever that's supposed to mean."

What a snob, thought Ant.

His silence compelled the professor to keep digging a proverbial hole for himself.

"Anyway, this young man has destroyed the remains of a valuable artefact. It might be argued that such items are common on villa digs, but that's not the point. It is the context which matters and what the discovery may have meant for the dig as a whole. Note I use the past tense, since the item is no more: it no longer exists."

Sounds like Monty Python's *parrot sketch to me*, thought Ant as he watched the professor's face flush in response to his widening grin. Ant could see the academic was tempted to bite back, but the thought of offending his benefactor wisely prevailed.

"Well, in the scheme of things, a broken lump of baked clay isn't too important at the moment is it, Professor?"

Unable to take his ire out on Ant, the professor turned his attention to the undergraduate, who had just finished picking up all the shards he could find.

"Take them to the finds tent. Record location, material, and design in the prescribed manner. I assume even you can do that?"

Ant watched the young man narrow his eyes then quickly lower his head. As he did so, the neck cover of his canvas desert cap rippled in the light breeze of a warming day.

Dismissing the interlude with the professor and his errant student, Ant returned his attention to the body that lay at his feet. He surveyed the scene, just as he had done too many times on active service.

He still found it distasteful.

"With all due respect, might I suggest you leave that to the police, Anthony?" said the professor, his voice indicating his subordinate position in their relationship.

Ant continued with his work as if no words were spoken. After judging sufficient time had elapsed to reinforce the pecking order, he lifted his gaze to the bespectacled head peering over the trench.

"Could it be you are more interested in me not damaging your excavation than any sympathy you might have for this poor soul?" Ant's intonation was flat.

The professor chose not to reply; there wasn't any point. Instead, he withdrew without comment, leaving Ant to ponder the quietness and odd contrast of a cloudless sky overhead and death at his feet.

Within a minute of the professor leaving, Lyn reappeared. She looked down on Ant with a mixture of sorrow and admiration.

"Routing around a corpse is not my idea of a fun day out."

Ant rolled his shoulder back so he could glimpse his friend without moving his position over the body.

"At least this one is fresh—and in one piece."

He could see Lyn was shocked at his matter-of-fact description of the body.

Before either had chance to pursue the topic, the harsh sirens of police cars approaching at speed startled both friends.

Hell, it's happening again, thought Ant as he curled up at lightning speed and clasped a hand to each ear.

"You okay?" said Lyn, her concern obvious.

Ant ignored his friend. It took him the best part of a minute to unfurl himself from his foetal position. He deliberately chose not to offer Lyn any eye contact. Instead, he stepped away from the body and climbed out of the trench. A spray of dust gave his presence away to a fast-approaching policeman.

"What are you doing in that trench? Viscount Stanton, is it not?"

The voice was authoritative.

Both turned towards the man.

Not from around here, thought Ant.

"Detective Inspector Riley," said the man, his voice laced with irritation.

"You're not local?" said Lyn.

The detective glanced into the trench before turning his attention back to Lyn.

"Correct. On detachment from Suffolk. Not that that's any concern of yours, miss."

Riley emphasised the word "miss." His taunt failed to trigger any reaction from Lyn, much to the detective's annoyance.

"And as for you, sir?" enquired Riley. "It may be your family's land, and in a way your professional territory, but why did you find it necessary to contaminate a possible crime scene?"

He's done his homework, thought Ant.

Aware he was on thin ice, Ant trod with care.

"You're right, Inspector. I should have known better, but I thought I saw movement and wanted to check if there was anything we could do for the poor chap. He is... or was... one of my father's employees. Noblesse oblige, and all that, you know."

It was all Lyn could do to stop herself from laughing. She knew Ant was playing with the detective.

"I see," he said, scratching his head. "Then perhaps the gracious Viscount Stanton could indulge a humble policeman and give him the benefit of his wisdom. Is the gentleman in question dead? Or is he afflicted? Perhaps derived from the strong smell of whisky in the air, which prevents him from closing his eyes when looking directly at the sun?"

Both looked skyward.

Ant adopted an exaggerated look of angst, varying his gaze between the body and the detective.

"Inspector. I think I know where you're coming from. No one, not even a drunkard, could look at that sun without blinking, could they?"

Riley wasn't impressed.

Ant continued his act.

"He's dead. That being the case I need to cancel the man's tenancy as of today. This will allow me to get his tied cottage ready for a new occupant."

He hadn't finished with Riley yet.

"And in future, please endeavour to use my correct title. As a courtesy to my father's title I am addressed as Lord Stanton."

He turned from the policeman and sauntered back towards his quad bike.

Lyn followed without comment.

Riley looked on as the pair left, unsure if his view of the aristocracy had been reinforced, or he'd been the butt of Ant's peculiar sense of humour.

Either way, he didn't like it.

4

WALK THE TALK

Unsure whether to laugh or scold Ant for the way he'd treated the detective, Lyn leant forward and shouted into Ant's right ear as the quad bike roared over the open grasslands of Alder Meadow.

"What was all that guff about tied cottages and tenancies? You sounded like a toff from *Downtown Abbey*."

"Sorry, can't hear you. What did you say?" shouted Ant as he revved the bike's engine.

Lyn responded by flicking the back of Ant's neck. Her perfectly manicured nail made its presence known. Unwilling to risk a second stab of pain, he brought the machine to a gradual halt on the crest of what passed for a hill in Norfolk.

"What was that for?" protested Ant, as he dismounted the bike while rubbing his neck.

It was now a competition to see who would break eye contact first. As usual, Lyn won.

"That fool Riley knew who I was. He's also aware of what I do for a living. If he had issues with either, it's not my fault, is it!"

Lyn half turned and feigned interest in a wherry sailboat gliding along Stanton Broad.

"And you're happy to play the arrogant, rich chap from the big house, are you?"

He smiled.

She frowned.

"Look, I'll play any role our detective friend assigns me. It suits my purpose for him to think me an inbred aristocrat. With luck, he'll leave us in peace to get on with things."

Lyn's frown deepened.

"If you're not careful, you'll stick like that," said Ant. "Remember what they say about frightening horses and children—and you deal with a lot of children!"

Lyn held up all ten fingernails as a friendly warning to Ant.

"Okay, I surrender. I'll do you a deal. You keep those nails to yourself, and I'll tell you what I found."

Lyn blew air across her fingers as she preened a nail tip.

"I think I've made my point, but what the heck are you on about?"

Unable to resist the temptation to keep Lyn waiting, he helped her off the bike and led her down to the edge of the Broad. They watched the wherry as it sailed around a bend. Soon all they could glimpse was its sail peaking above the reeds.

"Do you remember the times we spent on the boat when we were kids?" he asked.

Lyn smiled at the memory.

"I see now why your father called her *Field Glider*. You know it hadn't occurred to me until this second. Just look at the canvas float through the meadow. Wonderful sight, don't you think?"

A few minutes passed as the pair watched the slow-flowing water and pond skimmers dancing across its glinting surface.

"Come on, Ant. Get on with it," said Lyn.

He lay back on the baked grass, closed his eyes, and drank in the sun's warming rays.

"The land agent. It wasn't an accident. I'm sure of it."

Lyn waited for more. Instead, only silence.

"But he was drunk. And the stone... He landed on it, didn't he?"

Again, he made her wait.

"Well... yes... and, er, maybe. Or to be more exact, no and yes. I mean maybe."

"What?"

Lyn's tone warned Ant it was time to explain.

"Well, as for the whisky, yes, it was all over him, and I mean *over* him. But not the slightest whiff from his mouth?"

Lyn shook her head in exasperation.

'But you told the inspector he—"

"I played the part the man wanted me to play. As for the stone, yes, it caused his death, but he didn't fall onto the thing. Someone gave him one hell of a clout then placed it beneath his head once he was in the trench."

Lyn was having none of it.

"Hang on. I could smell the whisky even from where I was standing, and I heard what you said to the inspector.

Ant nodded his head in agreement.

"Yes, but he, or she, made a mistake. The bottom of that excavation was as clean as a whistle from the work the university bods had done. Why was that particular stone left? The murderer was too clever by half. Yes, the stone used to kill him was placed correctly; even the blood spatter matched Narky's head injury."

Lyn's mind was racing.

"Perhaps in the scuffle he knocked it into the trench then fell onto it, I suppose."

Ant shook his head.

"Good point, but why only that stone? No lumps of soil. No other rubbish in the bottom of the trench. No, believe me, he was poleaxed, and down he went like a sack of spuds. Then the killer placed the stone to make it look like Narky fell onto it."

Ant watched Lyn frown as she weighed up both theories.

"You see that stone sat on top of the soil? No depression, no movement from where it may have been originally. It just sat there. Fair enough if the thing had been half buried with the sharp end sticking out of the ground. But that wasn't the case. Now, if a bloke as heavy as Narky fell the best part of five feet, wouldn't you expect the stone to shift at least a little, or create a slight depression in the surface of the soil?"

Lyn nodded. It was time to concede, at least for now.

"Come on, Sherlock. Let's walk back to the Hall while I demolish your theory. I'm sure you can get one of the estate workers to bring the bike back."

Lyn waved a loose arm at the machine as she spoke.

Ant took little persuading.

"You're on. Come on, last one to the top of the hill makes the tea."

Reaching the crest of the small ascent Lyn raised her arms in triumph.

"You need to get yourself fit, mate. I thought the army were the best of the best."

Ant arrived a few seconds later shaking a hand in disagreement.

"As usual, you cheated. You started running before I'd finished talking."

Lyn laughed.

"I've heard everything now. At least you didn't say you let me win like you did when we were kids."

Ant lifted his chin and sniffed the air.

"I have nothing more to say on the matter, except, look at that. Isn't it beautiful?"

Ant's attempt to change the direction of the conversation worked as Lyn turned to join Ant looking down and into the mid distance.

"You're right. The Hall sits so wonderfully in its landscape. And to think your family has owned it for over two hundred and fifty years. Astonishing!"

Ant let out a gentle sigh.

"But for how much longer, I wonder?"

Lyn gave one of his arms a gentle stroke then playfully pushed him sideways with her shoulder.

"Come on, misery pants. No more of that. You may be many things, Anthony Stanton, but a quitter you are not."

Ant picked up on Lyn's encouraging smile. It was enough to lift any momentary doubts he had about the Hall's future.

'Oi! That hurt," replied Ant as he returned her smile and hurried to catch up with her.

"Oh, do shut up, and stop being a softie. Now let me get this straight. Narky wasn't drunk; someone perfumed him with spirits. He didn't fall; the same person clobbered him and pushed him into the trench. Then they went to the effort of making it look as if he'd fallen in a drunken stupor and hit his head on a small rock. Why? It makes no sense."

Ant nodded as the pair sauntered toward Stanton Hall.

"I agree, Lyn, but there are murderers who panic and leave clues all over the place. Others are more cunning, calculating. Almost fastidious in what they do."

By now the pair were approaching the west gate of the Hall. Ant had a surprise for his friend.

"And to prove my point regarding the meticulous murderer, there's this."

Ant slipped a small, folded piece of paper from his trouser pocket and handed it over.

"Careful, it's evidence."

Lyn unfolded the object as if it were a sheet of gold leaf.

"Good Lord."

"I know, but just read it," replied Ant.

I KNOW what you're up to and have the proof. If you don't leave us alone, you'll get what's coming to you, understand? Back off, or else.

"WHO DO you think wrote it? Where did you find it?"

Ant took the note back.

"Scrunched up in one of Narky's hands. It took a lot of working loose, let me tell you: rigor mortis and all that."

Lyn conjured up a mental picture of the scene. She didn't like it.

"As for the author, well, it's on estate-headed paper. And see these blotches? If you whiff them there's just a hint of methylated spirit."

Ant held out the note so that Lyn could see, or rather smell, for herself.

"Suppose so," she said. "So who's your painter?"

Ant shook his head.

"Not a painter, Lyn. Unless I'm mistaken, turpentine is a key part of French polish, and Glen Dawson has been renovating bookcases in the library."

Lyn couldn't hide her admiration for Ant's deductive skills, though she would have cut her right arm off rather than admit it to him.

"Isn't he the estate carpenter?"

"Yes, which means I have a responsibility towards him."

Lyn stared at Ant in disbelief.

"But he may be a murderer. It's not a game we're playing here. We need to tell the police before they find out and come after you for obstructing a police enquiry."

Ant grinned.

"Don't worry, I'll turn on the charm."

"Charm? Riley thinks you are an upper-class twit. It never worked with the class bully; remember him? It won't wash with that bully of a detective either. He's no fool, you know."

Ant accepted the admonishment, pushing the open palms of his hands forward.

"Mea culpa. I'll take the risk, Lyn. I won't let the police near Glen until I've made sense of this mess. And before you go off on one again, you'd do the same if it was one of your ex-pupils, and don't tell me any different. I know you too well."

"You mean *we'll* take the risk."

"As you say, old girl."

Ant waited for the fuse he'd lit to go off before sprinting forward and escaping through an open doorway before Lyn could land the wallop heading his way.

THE EARL SAT in the oak-panelled library of the great house as he bit into Lyn's cake. He lapped any filling that escaped and congratulated himself on consuming every morsel.

Outside in the corridor, Ant and Lyn continued their discussion as to who might have murdered Narky.

"Anyway, one thing is for sure. We need to crack on before Riley comes sniffing around here. Better bring Dad up to speed. Come on, he'll be in here."

Ant turned a large brass knob and pushed the heavy oak door open.

“I see you two have met up again. I also see you are still daft as brushes when you're together.”

Ant and Lyn exchanged an embarrassed glance before increasing the distance between them.

"Afternoon, Dad. I see you've found Lyn's cake. Any good?"

Ant gave Lyn a sideways glance. As he expected, she didn't think much of his comment.

"Careful, Son. If you want any of Lyn's excellent cake you need to watch out. Right, Lyn?"

"Absolutely. Sharp tongues are likely to go without."

The nearest Ant came to admitting defeat was to cut two slices of cake and offer one to Lyn.

"I'll take that as an apology, then. Shall I?"

The earl laughed, spitting bits of cream into the atmosphere as he did so.

"Mum will kill you, Dad."

The earl held a finger to his lips and gave them both a wide-eyed smile.

"Anyway, to what do I owe the pleasure of your company this fine day?"

Ant's demeanour became more serious. It was time to break the bad news and spent the next ten minutes explaining the events of the morning.

“What next, then? I assume you will not leave it to the police.”

“Spot on, Dad. I’m heading over to Glen's place. Are you coming, Lyn?”

She was ahead of him.

“No. I want to take another look around the dig site. You never know what might turn up.”

"Okay, but make sure you don't trip over the police tape and end up in that trench yourself. It'll be a giveaway to Riley that you've trampled all over his crime scene."

Ant noted Lyn's dismissive smirk. He winked at his father.

The earl gave each an affectionate smile as he gestured for them to get on with their investigation.

5

A BETTING MAN

I *love September*, thought Lyn as she strolled back to the dig site.

The busy landscape of farmers gathering in the harvest and tourists larking around on their hire boats made her heart race as she recalled the happy times of her early childhood racing across cropped fields and waving innocently to smiling holidaymakers as they sailed by.

A mosaic of fields ranged in colour from the deepest green to vivid yellow. A scattering of flint-faced churches and brick windmills pierced the flatlands, the latter now without their sails but no less glorious.

The scene triggered painful memories too. It was to this place that she came as a teenager when her parents' constant squabbling got too much.

Lyn thought about her early relationship with Ant. She smiled as she crossed a field of barley, their ripened ears tickling Lyn's knees as she waded through the golden crop.

What a pair we made. Me escaping my parents arguing, Ant trying to make sense of his privileged background.

When Lyn reached the excavations, all was quiet, other

than the sound of two muffled voices coming from the professor's tent.

Careful not to make her presence known, Lyn detoured around a cluster of temporary buildings. Within sixty seconds she'd reached the trench Narky was found in.

Tempted, though she was, to duck under the police tape and jump into the excavation, she resisted.

If Ant found nothing else of interest and the police cleaned it out, I guess I won't uncover any new stuff either.

Instead, Lyn concentrated on an area around a nearby spoil heap. She reasoned the murderer might have hidden behind it then jumped Narky.

Her plan proved fruitless. She was about to call it a day when something caught her eye. On the ground, midway between the excavation and the spoil heap, a small object stood proud against the sandy-grey colour of the compacted earth.

It was black with jagged edges.

Part of a thermos flask cup? Lyn thought.

Lyn studied the odd-shaped item, applying a level of care the professor might give to a precious find.

No, the radius of the curve was too big for a cup, but what else might it be? she thought.

Then a clue.

"VK."

On the outside of the curve, Lyn could make out two large letters. A maker's mark, perhaps? No, the letters had been hand painted and not by the hand of an expert.

The owner's initials, perhaps? thought Lyn.

"Ah, Glen. Glad I've caught you. Could I have a word?" said

Ant as he shuffled over to a man tightening the handle of a yard brush.

Surprised at the unexpected visitor, Glen Dawson laid the broom against a nearby water butt.

"Mr Anthony. They said you were back. Nice to see you."

Glen's voice was friendly enough, but it didn't conceal his nervousness.

"Nothing wrong. I was in the area and just wanted your advice on something, Glen."

Ant picked up on Glen's agitation.

Perhaps he had something to hide? thought Ant as he extended his hand.

"Oh, er, well, happy to help if I can, Mr Anthony. Please come into the house."

Glen shook Ant's hand then half turned towards a chocolate-box-looking estate cottage.

"I wish you would call me Ant."

Glen smiled nervously.

"Now, Mr Anthony, you know I've worked on the estate all my life, as did my grandfather and father before me. They taught me how to address the gentry."

Glen's response caught Ant off guard. He'd forgotten the effect a sudden visit by his father or him had on some of their long-standing tenants. Ant knew it was his responsibility to put Glen at ease, not the other way around.

"Sorry, Glen, that was tactless of me. Listen, whatever makes you feel comfortable, okay?"

Ant's touch of humility did the trick as he watched the hint of a smile spread across Glen's face and his shoulders drop.

"Oh, I see. Well, if you say so, er, Ant, but what Grandfather would say, I don't know."

Glen shook his head and lowered his gaze.

Ant knew he needed to move the conversation on without appearing to disrespect Glen's close family.

"Dad had told me what a fine chap your grandad was, and I know your father served the estate all his working life, but times change, Glen. And a good thing too. Wouldn't you agree?"

Ant's acknowledgement of his family's loyalty to the estate did the trick as he watched Glen's eyes meet his, together with a small, almost indiscernible, nod of the head.

Glen gestured for Ant to enter the open front door of his cottage. He shouted to Ruth, his wife.

The woman had none of the restraint her husband had shown. Instead, she welcomed Ant and offered to make refreshments.

Although Ant still suffered from the after-effects of eating too much of Lyn's chocolate cake, he was too much of a gentleman to refuse the woman's hospitality.

"Thanks so much. A cup of tea would be great. White with one sugar, if I may?"

Ruth smiled and disappeared into the kitchen, leaving the two men standing in the middle of the small room, its height made all the lower by an open-beamed ceiling.

"Please, Ant, take a seat. Now what's this advice you're after?"

Conscious he'd put Glen at ease under false pretences, Ant trod carefully. He'd undertaken enough interrogations to know how important it was to gain trust. That way he stood the best chance to get the information he needed.

"Well, you may think I'm being daft, but I had an argument about French polish with a friend the other day, and—"

"French polish?" Glen interrupted.

"Yes, I know, sounds silly, but I think white spirit is an important part of the mixture. My friend said I was wrong."

Glen shook his head and smiled.

"You know, a lot of tradesmen think that. The truth is, it's methylated spirit."

Ant feigned disappointment.

"Blast, that's cost me a tenner."

Ruth walked through from the kitchen holding a tray of tea.

"What's cost you a tenner?"

Ant shrugged his shoulders as Ruth handed him a delicate bone-china cup with matching saucer.

"A gift from your great grandmother, they were. It has been handed down the family and very proud to have them we are too."

Ant saw the pride with which she handled the precious objects and made sure he treated them with the greatest care.

"Well, Ruth, thanks to your husband, I've learnt to my cost about French polish and methylated spirit!"

Ruth scrunched her face up at the mere mention of the sticky concoction.

"Yuck. Can't stand the smell of that stuff. Glen's been doing work up at the big house, and it's been all over his clothes every day for a fortnight. Isn't that so, Glen?"

Her husband looked sheepish knowing he was in bad books with his wife for all the extra washing he'd caused.

Ant scrutinised Glen's reaction. It was playful. He observed no anxiety at the mention of meths.

Now it was time for Ant to show his cards. He hoped they'd forgive him, whatever happened.

"Bad do about Toby Collins, isn't it?"

The atmosphere changed in an instant. Glen tensed.

Ruth placed her cup back into its saucer with a clunk, not checking to see if she'd caused any damage.

"Narky, you mean. Yes, a bad do all right, but he was a bugger, Mr Anthony."

The reversion by Glen to formality told Ant he was onto something. He pressed his point home.

"The police are saying he fell in a drunken haze. Stank of whisky."

"Whisky?" replied Glen, his voice tinged with surprise.

"Not Narky," said Ruth. "That sod stuck to beer. Never touched spirits as far as I know. Every time he came round here he reeked of—"

Glen sprang from his chair to stand beside Ruth, taking her hand as he did so.

"Ant doesn't want to know about that, Ruthy. Let's not talk ill of the dead, eh?"

For the second time during their meeting, Ant felt uncomfortable. This wasn't like work. It was too close to home and involved people for whom he felt responsible.

"It's okay, Glen. I've been made aware of what he was like with the ladies. I'm sorry, Ruth. If my father had known what the man was like, he'd have sorted it. I promise you."

Ruth's hard exterior slipped. Her eyes glistened with emotion.

"There was nothing we could do without causing a fuss. None of us wanted that. Instead, us girls learnt how to handle the creep."

The show of raw emotion threw Ant, but he knew he had to get the truth out of Glen before the police picked up on the gossip.

"Glen. There's something I have to ask you, and I understand why you—"

Glen cut across Ant.

"You mean did I kill Narky for bothering Ruth? No, and that's the truth. Some of us lads hated the man, but as far as I know no one touched him."

Ant watched as Ruth gave her husband a look he'd often seen his own parents share. Proof of an unbreakable bond and a deep love in no need of words to explain it.

"The thing is, Glen, there's this..."

Ant handed over the piece of paper he'd taken from Narky's corpse.

Glen accepted the unwanted gift without surprise. Instead of reading it, he raised the note to his nose.

"Methylated spirit. That's why you came. You didn't lose a bet, did you, Mr Anthony?"

A coldness now permeated the room. Ant's hosts shot him the hardest of stares.

"It's true, Glen. I'm sorry. As you say, there was no bet. But I found that note in Narky's clenched hand—before the police had chance to crawl all over his body."

The pair separated and looked at each other in panic. Ant thought he was about to get a confession.

"I told you not to put anything in writing, Glen. Now look what's happened. When the police—"

"But nothing happened, love. "I know it was stupid to write the letter, but I didn't know what else to do. I did not kill that nasty sod. You have to believe me, my love."

Ruth glared at her husband.

"Tell that to the police, Glen. See what they say."

Ant intervened.

"Look, the police aren't coming, at least not yet. But Glen, you must tell me what happened."

Glen slumped back into his chair and stared down onto the footworn stone floor.

"He was blackmailing us. That's the truth of it."

Ant glanced at Ruth then fixed his stare on Glen.

"But why?"

Glen looked towards his wife. She nodded without saying a word.

"He wanted me to get involved in his scam. He found out Dad has a gambling habit, and we were desperate for money to pay his debts."

Glen lowered his head.

Ant struggled to make sense of Glen's explanation.

"Scam... What scam? And your dad?"

"Dad's got a dodgy kidney. The silly old bugger's drunk like a fish all his life, and he's bedbound now. Hates not being able to get into his garden. Anyway, he played bingo on an old laptop we had hanging around for a couple of years. I didn't even know he knew how to work the damn thing. It was only pennies a game at first. We didn't know anything about it. Then the bailiffs arrived. Narky overheard me telling a mate in the Wherry Arms and collared me. He said if I countersigned false invoices to the estate he'd generated from fictitious building contractors, he'd pay off Dad's debts."

At least he now understood why the estate was in such a financial mess.

"And before you ask," Glen continued, "no, I didn't. I refused, point-blank. So he came to the cottage bothering Ruth. I wrote that note saying I'd tell your father if he didn't stop. We wanted him out of our lives, but I didn't kill him. Honest to God, I didn't."

The room fell silent, with only the sound of an ancient long-case clock making its presence known. After seconds, which felt like hours to Ant, he responded.

"Glen, I believe you, and the police won't hear any of this. They don't know the note exists, and that's the way it'll stay. Now who holds your father's debt? Give me the name of the company and I'll sort it."

"But—" he said.

"But nothing. And if the police turn up, tell them about Narky pestering Ruth but nothing more. They'll have picked up the same response from around the village, so they won't have any reason to dig further, will they?"

6

SPEAKING IN TONGUES

Lyn finished pouring herself a generous glass of Prosecco before wandering onto the patio to take in the early evening breeze.

The old schoolhouse was a building she passed on her way to class every day as a child. She always wondered what inside might be like. Now she owned it.

It had been a struggle, but the borrowed view onto farmland at the end of the back garden had swung it.

Strange how life turns out, she thought.

Things couldn't be more different now. Instead of acting as a gofer between her mother and father, she was in charge of her life.

Sure, it was a small village and impossible to do much without someone noticing, but Lyn saw no reason to move.

The foibles of village life soon melted away as Lyn settled into a comfy recliner. She placed her drink on a low glass tabletop and picked up her book of the moment.

Nothing better than a good historical romance, she thought.

But try as she did, the events of the past twenty-four hours kept niggling.

She knew the reputation Narky had, although she'd never met the man. No matter how he behaved, she knew no one deserved to die like that.

Doubting she'd make much progress with her book, Lyn popped it back on the table and picked up her wine. As she sipped from a tall glass and gazed out across the meadow, she noticed a group of people in a huddle.

Curiosity having got the better of her, Lyn returned the Prosecco to the table and passed into the meadow via a low gate in the hedge.

"Found anything interesting?" she said, engaging three metal detectorists and explaining her own interest in history.

"I'm Lyn, by the way. I live in the house just over the hedge."

The three strangers looked over Lyn's shoulder towards the old schoolhouse before returning Lyn's friendly smile.

"I'm Sid, the oldest and most intelligent of our little band, and the daft-looking one to my left is young James. We're here for a weekend rally just up the road, and the organiser got us permission to detect the meadow."

Lyn shook Sid's hand before turning her attention to the teenager.

"Let me guess, he's your father?"

Lyn picked up on the twinkle in the lad's eyes.

"Thought so."

Sid pointed at a young woman wearing what Lyn assumed to be the obligatory uniform of detectorists, comprising of camouflage jacket and trousers, stout boots, and oversized bobble hat.

"And finally, we have Sandy. She's just dug an Eddy One, silver hammered, lucky sod."

The strange terminology baffled Lyn.

"Hammered Eddies? What on earth are you talking about?"

The detectorists looked at each other then laughed. Lyn just looked puzzled.

"Well," said Sandy as she pulled a small plastic box from a hip pouch, "look here." Lyn watched as the woman delicately picked out a small silver disc with gloved fingers and placed it into the palm of her free hand.

"This is a silver penny. Struck in Winchester in the reign of Edward the First, I'd say. That would make it thirteenth century. Isn't that amazing?"

Lyn couldn't help but notice Sandy's face light up as she explained her find.

"And the 'hammered' bit?"

"They were made by placing a disc of silver on a metal die, with its matching pair placed on top. Then—wallop! A big bloke with a good swing 'hammered' the die to stamp the design and make it legal tender."

Lyn smiled.

"Ah, I see, makes perfect sense. Could I ask you a huge favour? Would you like to show off your metal-detecting skills to the kids at my school sometime? They'd love it."

"Your school?" said Sid.

"Sorry, I should have said I'm head teacher at Stanton Primary, and I'm guessing the thought of finding treasure will more than keep my young charges' attention."

The detectorists exchanged glances with no need to discuss the request.

"Great idea, as long as you have a go first!" Sid replied.

Before Lyn had chance to answer, he slid the headphones over her ears and handed over the metal detector.

"That's it, swing it slow and low. Good technique; you're a natural!" he exclaimed as Lyn ambled forward, her ears filled with beeps and grunts as the machine distinguished between different types of metal.

Lyn was in her element, and before long she'd picked up a high-pitched, bright-sounding signal.

"Let me listen," said Sid as he cupped an ear to the earphones. "You've got something all right."

A few minutes of digging in the rock-hard soil produced a neat hole, at the bottom of which something glistened. Lyn knelt and scraped around the small object. Finally, the ground gave up its hostage.

An aluminium ring pull.

"Congratulations on your first find. Circa last year, I'd say. Don't worry, we find more of this stuff: bits of old iron and bullets rather than coins, let alone gold and such like!"

Lyn examined the shiny object as if it were a rare medieval treasure.

"Here, let me help you untie yourself," said Sid as Lyn handed back the headphones and undid the arm strap that held the detector in a comfortable position.

As Sid retrieved the machine, she glimpsed the armrest properly for the first time.

That's it, she thought.

The broken shard she'd found at the dig site matched the shape of the support.

"What an amazing coincidence," said Lyn. "I found a piece of one of these the other day." She pointed to the armrest.

"Do you know anyone with the initials 'VK'?"

The trio looked puzzled for a moment, then it dawned.

"Vikki King. She's in our club," said Sid.

Lyn knew she was chancing her arm.

"Any chance of putting me in touch with her? Just something I want to talk to her about," said Lyn.

"We can beat that. Vikki's with us on the rally. We've got a BBQ later tonight. We'll introduce you if you fancy a soggy beef burger!"

THE FIELD WAS HEAVING with detectorists as Lyn pulled onto the campsite. Making her way through the throng, she strained her eyes to see any of the trio she'd spent a pleasant thirty minutes with earlier in the evening.

"Lyn, glad you could come."

The voice was hard to pinpoint above the hubbub, but a friendly hand on her shoulder made her turn. Sid's smiling face greeted her.

"Hi, I'd never have found you in this lot. I didn't know metal detecting was so popular."

Before Lyn could continue the conversation, she reached for her mobile. It was Ant. The din and poor reception made it impossible to hear him, other than something about new information. Then nothing. She tried ringing back twice. His news would have to wait.

Breaking through the crowd, Sid came to a halt in front of a woman standing by a burger bar.

"Vikki, there you are. This is Lyn, the lady I mentioned earlier."

Lyn sensed the woman was nervous.

"Thanks for agreeing to see me. Did Sid explain why I wanted to meet with you?"

The woman failed to take Lyn's extended hand.

"I've done nothing wrong. We all have permission to be on the land. Not everyone likes metal detectorists, you know. I assumed you wanted to have a go at me."

Lyn smiled.

"Do you think I'd mix it with you lot if I wanted to have a go?"

Lyn waved her arms at the throng to make her point, still smiling.

Lyn could see her acknowledgement of the busy camp had helped Vikki relax.

"Suppose not."

The two spent a few minutes talking about safe subjects. Lyn, about how her pupils would love to try their hands at detecting, and Vikki, about getting sore feet and swollen knees digging the hard ground. Lyn tried to judge her next move, knowing Vikki might take flight.

"You know, when I was at the dig site yesterday, I found something. I think it was a piece of a metal detector. It had the initials 'VK' on it—"

Vikki cut Lyn off midsentence.

"That's why you're here." Vikki's nostrils flared as she looked in vain for Sid who was now lost in the crowd.

Lyn tried hard to calm the young woman, but she was having none of it.

"Look, I'm no nighthawk, okay? I told you, we all have permission to be on the land."

Lyn looked confused. She'd never heard the term.

"Nighthawk? What in heck's name is that?"

Vikki folded her arms as if defending her private space.

"Illegal, so-called detectorists who work the fields for finds after dark. No permission, no insurance, and they don't belong to a professional body. We hate them cos they get us all tarred by the same brush. It's not fair."

Lyn could see Vikki felt strongly. Emotions were running high, and she needed to reassure the woman.

"Listen, I haven't a clue what you're on about, and I'm not accusing you of anything. I just need to find out how that piece of plastic ended up near the spoil heap, that's all."

Vikki's arms remained tightly folded.

"Two of us were asked to check the spoil heap again by that professor bloke, to see if any metal artefacts had slipped through. My mate didn't show up, and since I was already there, I detected alone."

Lyn sensed now was the time to push things.

"What happened? I can see from your expression that something upset you."

Lyn watched as Vikki scanned the crowd as if playing for time. *Why the hesitation?* thought Lyn.

"I swiped him one, okay?" Her eyes bored into Lyn, nostrils flaring.

Lyn wasn't sure how she felt. Elated? Scared?

Was Narky's murderer standing right in front of her?

God, what now? she thought.

"Who did you swipe, Vikki?" was all she could muster.

Vikki's eyes widened.

"I can tell this is upsetting for you, and I'm sorry. I just want to help. But to do that I need to know what happened up there."

Lyn sensed Vikki's dilemma. She knew from her own experience of the need to talk when something bad happened. Vikki wanted, needed, to tell someone what she had done.

Vikki started to shake. Lyn's instinctive reaction was to hug her. It worked.

"I didn't hang around to find out. All I know is a bloke came at me. I didn't hear him at first because of my earphones. I swung my metal detector at him, and he fell. Then I legged it. It was only after that I discovered I'd broke the armrest."

"I hope he's okay. I didn't mean to hurt him, but he scared the life out of me."

Lyn tried to reassure Vikki, but her expression must have given the game away.

"He's not, is he? Are you the police? Is he in hospital?" Vikki blurted.

Lyn released Vikki and pulled back a little. She tried to pick her words carefully, but there was only one way to say it.

"A man died up there on Saturday morning, Vikki. I'm sorry."

As she spoke, her mobile rang again. Lyn fumbled in her jacket pocket and tried to silence the phone.

When she looked up, Vikki had disappeared.

7

LUNCH FOR TWO

Sunday morning introduced itself with a heavy layer of low cloud and the threat of rain.

Bet it throws it down today. Why does it always seem to rain on a Sunday? Lyn thought.

Even the pleasure of sipping the first strong coffee of the day did little to lift her mood as she looked at the leaden sky through her kitchen window.

At least my parents can't chuck me out in the garden anymore while they argue, she thought.

It seemed the more successful Lyn's career became, the more her thoughts turned back to her childhood. She knew one day she'd have to confront her demons.

"Are you seeing Lyn today, Son?"

His father had a glint in his eye as Ant pushed the wheelchair through a tall pair of French doors and out onto a paved terrace.

"The gardens are looking good, Dad," said Ant as he surveyed the formal lines of box hedges and dense planting of lavender.

"It's September, and the lavender is going over, as you well know. Stop trying to change the subject."

Ant knew his father would refuse to be distracted by his sudden interest in horticulture and pondered the knack parents had in turning their adult offspring back into children.

He tried to deflect the question, though he didn't know why he felt the need to do so.

"Dad, you've been trying to marry us off since we were eighteen. It's not going to happen. What sort of chap falls for a girl who was his security detail at school? A bit embarrassing, don't you think?"

The elderly gentleman chuckled, so much so that his shoulders heaved as he coughed.

"See what plotting does for you," said Ant as he bent over to check his father wasn't in any real distress.

"Don't worry, Anthony, it's not another heart attack. You're safe for now. Anyway, bodyguards come in handy no matter what age you are. You, above anyone, should know that."

Ant knew that in one sentence his father had made light about his own health, the estate's future, Ant's military service, and his relationship with Lyn. That was his father's style. Ant admired his brevity, even if the Earl of Stanton's words made him uncomfortable about his past and future.

"I see you haven't lost your enthusiasm for mapping out my future, Dad. I understand my responsibilities, and I'm not talking about Lyn. She's an adult and knows her own mind."

“Well, one of you has to, I suppose,” replied Ant’s father, his face beaming.

Ant shook his head in playful response as they spent a few minutes taking in the open landscape that surrounded Stanton Hall.

Interrupting the silence, Ant asked the question that was the real purpose of his visit.

"That was a bad do up at the dig site, wasn't it?"

Ant's father nodded.

"Have you found anything out yet? I'll lay a bet it's not just those metal detectorists who are doing some digging. Come on, tell me what you've discovered."

Ant's smile dissolved.

“I found out that our land agent had been fleecing us for years, Dad. Did you know?”

Ant watched his father hesitate and play for time by jabbing the armrest of his wheelchair with his index finger.

“I knew something was wrong but couldn't put my finger on it. The accounts seemed to balance, and he always behaved impeccably to your mother and me. I assumed he was a good sort of chap and loyal to us. However, year after year, cash went out faster than it was coming in, and I just couldn't understand it. I had intended to speak to you, Son."

Ant sensed his father visibly shrink in his wheelchair as the truth dawned.

"The truth is, the more I find out about Narky, the more unpleasant and calculating a thug he turns out to have been. It seems he found a way, or stumbled across, a means of siphoning off cash from the estate and intimidating anyone who got in his way, or whose compliance he needed. He was the one in control of events, Dad, so he could act any part he wanted in front of Mum and you, so don't be too hard on yourself. We'll find a way of putting this place on a firm footing."

Ant's father rallied as he listened.

"And recent events have rather dealt with the matter, don't you think?"

Ant knew his father had picked his words with care.

"That's one way of looking at things, Dad. But I need to be sure certain people are telling me the truth. Otherwise, Narky's death may remain unresolved and the estate's future in danger."

Ant's father nodded then shocked his son by doing something he'd never done before.

"Give your father a hug."

Ant instinctively bent over the earl and gently folded his arms around the elderly man's delicate shoulders until their heads kissed each other's cheek. After a few seconds, his father patted Ant's back as a signal he understood well.

Sitting on a curved stone bench to the side of his father's wheelchair, Ant sensed the earl wanted to say something to him.

"Is everything all right, Dad?"

His father frowned and looked earnestly at Ant.

"I know this probably isn't the moment to raise the subject, but truth be told, Anthony, it's all getting too much for your mother and me." The elderly man gave his armrest one last stab with his finger before adding, "There. I've said it."

Relaxing back into his chair, having spoken the words he'd needed to voice for a long time, his agitation eased.

Ant's shock at finally hearing the words he dreaded was no less for it actually happening.

Why do we think our parents will live forever? thought Ant.

"I hesitated all this time because of the pressure I knew

you would feel in sacrificing your military career and having to return home. And for what? A life mending dilapidated buildings and fending off the day when the estate might have to go over to the National Trust: lock, stock, and leaking roof. And on top of that, this Narky business and all the damage he's done to us."

Ant pushed the wheelchair back through the French doors and into a spacious drawing room without responding to his father's admission. He had just heard his father admit, perhaps for the first time in his life, that he couldn't cope.

The rich décor and family portraits that hung on each wall hit home as Ant reflected on his privileged background and the responsibility that went with it.

"But the main thing is, Anthony, that we get an expert in to help run things. Don't you agree?"

Ant's father didn't give him chance to respond.

"Now, let's have that cup of tea before you shoot off to see Lyn, and you must take back her cake tin." The Earl of Stanton spoke in a matter-of-fact way. Head buried in a book, his eyes anywhere but on his son.

Ant knew this wasn't the time to prolong his father's distress. At such times in his family, he knew a touch of light-hearted banter was called for. It was easier than confronting truths.

"My plans do not include seeing Lyn today, as you well know, Father. But seeing as you want that blessed cake tin returned to her, I will, indeed, take it."

Ant's father nodded, all the time pretending to read his book.

"As you say, Anthony. As you say."

"ALL RIGHT, all right, I'm coming," moaned Lyn as she made her way from the kitchen to the front door.

"My father said you wanted this back." Ant held out the cake tin. "And I wanted to check your telephone."

"Good morning to you too, Ant," replied a bemused Lyn, relieving her visitor of the tin. Since when have you been in the telephone maintenance business?"

Ant followed Lyn down the hall and into the kitchen.

"Since you stopped answering your phone. I wanted to fill you in on my meeting with Glen."

Lyn glanced at the handset on the granite worktop next to the fridge. It was flashing.

"Ah," said Lyn, before attempting to change the subject, "and I've got something important to tell you."

"Ah," replied Ant, as he perched himself on a bar stool.

Enjoying seeing Lyn squirm, he pushed home his advantage.

"Seeing as I made the trip over here just to bring the cake tin back, do I get lunch? Anyway, where were you last night? First you cut me off on the mobile, then you don't answer your home phone."

Lyn threw a well-aimed tea towel at Ant as she bent down to open the oven and retrieve a cottage pie.

Ant didn't bother ducking. Instead, he caught the towel, folded it into a neat square and hung it over the stool.

"So how does your news trump me seeing the carpenter? For all you know I could have found our murderer."

"Place mat," urged Lyn as she pointed to the worktop so she could put the piping-hot dish onto the dining table. Task accomplished, Lyn slipped off a pair of oven gloves and sat opposite him.

"Because I've found our murderer, that's why," she announced, trying hard to control her excitement.

Ant raised an eyebrow.

"You need not look so surprised, you know," she said, irritated he didn't take her news with the seriousness it deserved.

"Not at all," replied Ant. "You may well have, but don't forget Glen."

Ant explained the conversation he'd had with the carpenter and his wife.

"We know Narky was a bad lot, and although Glen's explanation seems plausible, I've one or two scars on my back from believing people I *wanted* to be innocent, so we shall see."

Ant could see Lyn's frustration as she realised there was a contender who might scupper her own theory. She lost no time in telling Ant about Vikki King and listed the case against the detectorist.

"She was there on the night Narky died, had a motive because she feared an attack, and Vikki *admitted* hitting 'someone.'"

Ant rose from the table and walked the short distance to the coffee machine, gesturing to Lyn if she'd like a drink.

"No thanks. Well, what do you think?"

Ant took in the rich aroma of the fresh coffee and took a sip.

"Not bad. Not bad at all. Where did you get it from?"

He watched as Lyn's face flushed. He knew what he was doing.

"Joke," he added to head off Lyn's fury.

"On the one hand a good defence lawyer will argue self-defence. On the other hand, a good council for the prosecution will press the jury for a guilty verdict on the basis that Narky was unarmed and drunk as a lord. Nevertheless, we need to speak to her, pronto. The police aren't far behind us, and they'll have a field day with the evidence you found."

Lyn began to draw imaginary sketches on the tablecloth with her finger.

"Is there a problem? I know when you are trying to avoid saying something."

Lyn withdrew her finger and looked over towards Ant.

"There's a slight problem. Vikki has disappeared."

"Clumsy of you, that," teased Ant. "Do you think she'll still be in the area?"

Lyn wasn't sure whether Ant was being sarcastic or asking a genuine question.

"I don't know, and I'm loath to tell Inspector Plod in case he messes it up."

Ant nodded.

"I'm with you on that, old thin—" he started.

Lyn picked up the tea towel, making ready to flick a corner at Ant.

"I've said before, don't you call me old... anything."

"Okay, okay, point made. Anyway, I'm agreeing with you, aren't I? So no more threats of violence, please."

Ant put on his best "little boy lost" look for added impact but could see Lyn remained unimpressed.

"All I'm saying is that we'd better get a move on if we want to catch up with your mysterious Vikki. That's if she's still around. The rally finishes in about two hours, you know."

A look of panic spread across Lyn's face as Ant's words hit home.

"Come on," said Lyn as she zipped across the kitchen and towards the front door. "Your car or mine?"

Ant looked crestfallen.

"Er... what about the cottage pie? I'm starving."

Ant pointed at the steaming food nestled in a gleaming Pyrex dish.

Lyn had already opened the car door.

"It'll keep," she shouted. "Slam the door on your way out; it sticks.

8

THE RACE IS ON

It was fortunate that Mini Clubman cars tended not to take up much space on the rural roads of Norfolk.

Any faster, and she'll have us in a ditch, Ant thought and considered themselves all the luckier for not having met a tractor coming the other way. Harvest time meant the huge machines hunted in packs. Ant held on for dear life and tried to banish memories of his brother's car accident.

Lyn's excited voice broke his depressive train of thought.

"There she is."

Lyn jabbed her finger towards a figure in the middle distance as the car approached the rally site.

"For the love of mercy, woman, slow down," Ant shouted as he grabbed a plastic handle just above the passenger door and braced himself. The vehicle shuddered as it completed a sudden swerve to the left.

"I've felt safer in a Challenger tank under fire than with you."

Lyn gave Ant a dismissive glance as she leant forward into the steering wheel.

"Made it," squealed Lyn as she brought the Clubman to a sliding halt within an inch of her target.

Ant took a few seconds to summon enough courage to open his eyes. As he did so, he noticed a crowd of onlookers dusting themselves down from a soil-laden vortex of air caused by Lyn's energetic driving.

"Thank you for such an uneventful ride, Lyn. Remind me to get the bus back, will you?"

It took Ant a little longer to loosen his grip on the handle above his head.

In front of Lyn's Mini, a startled Vikki King leant at a curious angle into the boot of her own car. She looked as though she was unsure whether to jump into it for safety or run for cover.

"Vikki, glad we caught you. This is my friend, Ant. It's his land you're on, and well, we want... that is, er, need..."

In her excited state, Lyn's words tumbled into one another.

Sensing she was in danger of doing more harm than good, Ant intervened.

"Hi, Vikki. What Lyn is trying to say is that she was so sorry to have lost sight of you last night, and could she have another word. Isn't that right, Lyn?"

Lyn didn't take to his tone, and Ant's failure to note her sternest head-teacher look further inflamed the situation. She could see his intervention had spooked Vikki as she watched the detectorist play with the shoulder straps of her backpack and avoid eye contact.

Lyn sensed it was time for everyone to take a breath and begin again.

The brief silence worked.

"About last night," said Vikki.

Lyn's eyes widened. She hoped for a confession.

"Sorry," Vikki continued, "Jed Bridges grabbed me. He's organised the rally and wanted to get pictures of my finds. When I got back, you were gone. I tried to find you but assumed you'd got fed up waiting for me."

Lyn's excitement faded as it dawned on her Vikki's explanation was plausible and that she might not be the murderer after all.

Why would the woman have hung around if she had intended to give me the slip last night?

The more Lyn mulled things over, the more ridiculous she felt. Catching Ant's glance, she knew he had already come to the same conclusion.

"And have you found anything of interest?" Ant asked in a well-practised manner.

Vikki let go of the backpack.

"Two Henry's. One hammered, a jetton, and a cut half. Oh, and a John one. So not bad for a weekend on hard, dry ground. Not much resistance for the detector to work on, you see."

"A what and a what?" replied Ant, baffled at Vikki's stream of gobbledygook.

She tried again.

"Well, a hammered is—"

Lyn interrupted.

"I'll explain later, Ant. Let's just say not a bad haul of handmade silver coins around eight hundred years old and a seventeenth-century French gaming counter. Now what about that man who attacked you at the dig site, Vikki?"

"Impressive or what," said Ant. "Been watching *Time Team*, have we?"

Vikki nodded. "Spot on, Lyn. Except that jettons were never official legal tender, more like—"

"Yes, yes, I know," replied Lyn, irritated at being corrected in front of Ant.

Lyn could see Ant enjoyed the moment and awaited further explanation, hoping she would make a mistake.

"No, I haven't watched that Tony Robinson bloke, I mean. And yes, I know all about jettons. A couple of Vikki's detectorist friends gave me a quick introduction to the hobby yesterday."

"Well, fair play, anyway. Then again, as a teacher, I suppose you're used to catching bits of information and presenting it back to your pupils as if you're a world expert." Ant's response was light hearted, but it hit the spot.

Lyn gave Ant one of her special stares reserved for only the worst behaved of her pupils.

They continued to exchange the barrage of insults only good friends can get away with without exchanging blows. Around them the hubbub of vehicles being loaded and driven off the field intensified.

In between giving and receiving playful insults, Lyn noticed Vikki was keen to join the exodus and had closed the boot of her car and belted herself into the driving seat.

She broke off from squabbling with Ant.

"Ah, you're keen to get away, I suspect. Have you far to drive?"

"Four hours if there aren't any holdups."

"Just a quick question, Vikki," said Lyn as she gathered her thoughts. "Is there anything else you can tell us about the man who attacked you? Anything at all?"

Vikki shook her head as she lifted her foot from the clutch pedal and pressed the accelerator.

"Sorry," she replied as her car started to move. "He came at me so fast I didn't see him. He was like a whippet."

With that she drove off, leaving the pair shrouded in a whirling mist of dry clay.

"Well, that's that. Now what do we do?"

Ant cleared the last of the dust from his lungs with a throaty cough and cast his eyes across the horizon. Lyn watched for some pearl of wisdom from her more experienced sleuthing partner.

"I think that the cottage pie you cooked should just about be the right temperature for eating, don't you?"

Lyn frowned.

"A murderer on the loose, and all you can think about is food."

9

REFLECTIONS

Ant crouched and covered his head with a soapy hand as Lyn dropped a Pyrex dish. It crashed onto the stone floor of her kitchen.

"That's the second time in three days you've reacted to a sudden noise like that," said Lyn. She tried hard not to show alarm.

Ant didn't answer at first. Instead, preferring to pick up individual clumps of soggy potato and mincemeat that had splattered all around them.

"I defy anyone not to jump when one of those shatters," replied Ant, having used the time before speaking to calm himself. "And you always were the clumsy one."

Lyn was having none of it.

"Don't change the subject, Anthony Stanton. Jump, yes. Cower, no. Now what's going on?" Lyn wasn't in the mood, and she could tell Ant knew it.

The pair continued to do the dishes in silence. Lyn washing. Ant drying.

Lyn had decided she wasn't going to let the matter drop.

After placing the last of the dried dishes in a pine plate rack, Lyn pressed the point.

"Come on, let's sit down."

She led her friend by the hand to the dining table.

"Now, please, talk."

Lyn studied his face closely as she sensed him struggle to find the words.

"Ant, look at me."

He did as he was told. She watched his eyes fill with tears, and he fought for the right words.

“PTSD. That's—"

Lyn gently interrupted and raised a hand to his cheek by way of reassurance.

"I know what post traumatic stress disorder is, Ant. Why haven’t you said anything before?"

She moved her hand to wipe away the faintest of tears from the corners of Ant's eyes.

Ant didn't move an inch except for fiddling with the salt cellar until Lyn covered his hand with hers and brought the circular movement to a halt.

“Not the sort of thing a military intelligence officer admits to, is it?” He offered no resistance to Lyn’s hand restraint.

“Why are you being so hard on yourself, Ant?” replied Lyn, her gentle tone doing its job in helping him relax. “I don’t know what you’ve seen on active duty, but if the news on the telly is anything to go by, I can imagine.”

Ant let out a short, sharp laugh as he threw his head back. He tried to stifle the sound. He didn’t mean to offend.

“Imagine? You've no idea. Only *we* know.” Lyn guessed his response conjured up images he'd rather not recall.

She had no answer to offer but sensed his unease was returning.

"It's okay, Ant. You're safe here."

Ant brought his head forward and met Lyn's eye contact.

"When I report back to the barracks, the shrinks want to assess me before they'll let me rejoin my unit. If things go belly up, you might be seeing a lot more of me. That means Dad's problem with running the estate will be sorted. Two birds killed with one stone, you might say."

His tone was more pragmatic now.

"If I sound a tad angry, I'm sorry. It's just I'd have preferred to pick my own time for packing the military in."

Lyn studied her friend. She didn't detect anger. In fact, just the reverse. He looked calm now, almost matter of fact. Lyn suspected he'd wanted to have this conversation for a long time.

Now it was her time to share.

"You know, when I was training to qualify as a teacher, they put me in a tough inner-city comprehensive in Hampshire. I got to know a teacher who'd worked there for over thirty years and had seen it all. He loved his job. The other teachers bribed the kids with treats to keep them quiet but not Graham. He went into the classroom, got on with his job, and do you know what? The kids loved him."

Ant put the salts down with the lightest of touches.

"So you're telling me a fairy tale about a superb teacher that every child in the world loved? What's that got to do with the price of fish?"

"Nothing," she said. "He told me that as a young teacher, he'd hit a brick wall after about twelve months in the job. He felt he couldn't live up to his own expectations and developed panic attacks. Then one day, for no particular reason, he sat on the floor in a corner of the classroom, put his head in his hands, and cried like a baby."

Ant cocked his head to one side.

"So was he a great teacher or a lousy one?"

"Neither," said Lyn. "It took six months on sick leave for him to accept what had happened. Then it clicked. He hadn't failed at anything; he got out of teaching for a few years and did other stuff until he felt ready to go back. Now he's in control. He deals with things as they are, not what might have been, or could be."

"And your point?" said Ant.

"Go with the flow," she replied as she slowly picked up the salt and tipped a gentle trickle of the white crystal onto the table.

Had anyone else said that he would have told them to stop patronising him. With Lyn, it was different. He had nothing to prove to her. He'd always acknowledged she knew him better than anyone.

"Look at the mess you've made," said Ant, his mood lifting in the safe company of his trusted friend.

"Maybe you're right," replied Ant as Lyn watched him carefully gather the salt into the palm of his hand. "But one thing's for sure. Sitting here won't find our killer, will it?"

Ant threw the salt he'd collected over his right shoulder and stood up. Lyn returned his broad smile. Her chair made a scraping sound as she moved it backwards over the stone floor.

"Time to visit the crime scene again, yes?"

"LORD, that fool of a detective is milling about up there. Better keep out of the way until he's gone," said Ant as Lyn brought her car to a stop on the edge of the dig site.

"You'd better move the Mini through that gate onto the farm track." Ant was pointing to an ancient, wooden structure held together with twine that nestled between two great elm posts. "If he comes back this way, he'll see us and will want to know what we're doing."

Get a move on, man, thought Ant as he watched the detective wander around the dig site kicking clods of earth, first with one foot then the other. *Looks like he's lost a pound and found a penny,* mused Ant as he looked at his watch. A further ten minutes passed before the policeman gave up, dusted himself down, and returned to his car.

"Do you think he found out about the broken metal detector?" said Lyn.

"Not a chance." Ant shook his head. "He'd have come for you quicker than a rat up a drain pipe if he'd cottoned onto anything like that."

Within a few seconds the detective's car had disappeared from the field.

"Better safe than sorry," said Ant as he leapt from their hiding place, clambered over a rickety wooden stile, and made off, leaving Lyn in his wake.

"Thank you for helping."

Ant gave a quick look over his shoulder. "Equality and all that. You can't have it both ways."

Lyn huffed.

Ant sensed he would pay for his comment at some point.

Seconds later, the pair stood over the trench, that until a few days previously, had cradled the body of Narky Collins. Now empty, Ant might have convinced himself that nothing had happened at all.

Then from behind, a muffled noise.

He went into automatic pilot. Hunching his back to make himself the smallest target possible as he made his way to the side of the spoil heap.

Ant gestured for Lyn to follow. She needed no encouragement.

Out of the gloom, Ant made out the shape of a tall, young man.

"Sorry to startle you. I'm Simon. I'm part of the team from the university."

Ant's shoulders dropped as he heaved a sigh of relief.

"Good God, man, you gave us the shock of our lives. What are you doing up here on a Sunday? It's almost dark."

Simon repeated his apology.

"I'm trying to get back into the professor's good books by seeing if any artefacts have made their way onto the spoil heap. It sometimes happens, you know."

The man's voice trembled. Ant could see he looked terrified.

"Hello, Simon," said Lyn. "No need to be scared. Not of us, anyway. As for your professor, well, that's another story. It's okay though. We won't tell."

Lyn's calming words did the trick. Simon's demeanour changed.

"It's so hard, you see. To get a full-time job in archaeology, I mean. I thought if I could make up for my mistakes, it might stand me in good stead, you know, with the professor."

After a few minutes of gentle conversation about what the university hoped to learn from the dig, Ant brought matters to a conclusion.

"Well, all I can say is, that based on what we've seen here this evening, the professor needs to know just how committed you are to your career."

Ant's words of encouragement had the desired effect. The young man smiled as he turned to leave.

"Oh, did you find anything?"

"Find anything?" replied Simon. Er, no. Not this time."

Then he was off with the neck protector from his cap fluttering in the light breeze.

Ant suggested they take a minute to reflect on the case so far.

"So we have a carpenter that threatened to expose Narky for trying to blackmail him but who seems to have a rock-solid alibi."

"And we have a metal detectorist up here that night who admits clobbering someone who, how did Vikki put it, 'ran at me like a whippet.'"

Both fell silent for a few seconds.

Ant broke the impasse.

"Back to basics. Let's see what the villagers have to say. Somebody must know something. This is Stanton Parva after all: the gossiping capital of East Anglia!"

Lyn laughed.

'In the meantime, I have the small matter of work to prepare for school tomorrow. Speaking of which, would you like to visit your old alma mater to catch up on the world of education?"

Ant groaned. "Must I?"

'I'll even throw in a free school dinner for you," added Lyn as she sped off back towards her car.

"Yuck," replied Ant, well out of earshot as he made up ground to catch up with his companion.

10

A CLASS ACT

Lordy Lord, doesn't everything look small, thought Ant as he wandered around the space in which he'd spent the first year of his school life.

"Wasn't sure if you would turn up, Ant." He watched Lyn as she strode in with a confident air about her and a cluster of children in her slipstream.

"Their teacher will be a few minutes late, so I'll just get them settled, then we can go over what we've found out so far."

Ant nodded as Lyn welcomed each child to the classroom and directed them to their seats as each gave Ant a curious stare.

"This is an ex-pupil, children, and this was his classroom when he was a little boy," Lyn explained.

Ant felt as though he were that little boy again and was certain he would sit on one of the miniature chairs if instructed to do so by the head teacher.

"Good morning, Joe. Did you have a good weekend?"

"Yes, miss," replied Joe as Lyn welcomed in the next child with a similar greeting.

Ant could see Lyn was in her element directing one child to hand out the exercise books, checking another had brought their gym pumps, and reminding a third to tie her footwear.

"We don't want to hit our head again, do we, Charlotte?"

"No, miss," replied the girl, bending down to tie her shoelace.

A few minutes later a dishevelled-looking young man tumbled into the room making the children giggle.

"Oh dear, my car broke down again, and I didn't have enough money for the bus, so I had to walk."

The teacher's explanation caused the children to giggle all the more as Lyn handed over the keys to the room and winked at the teacher.

Ant almost felt sorry for the man. However, the chance to escape the noise and general air of chaos tempered his sympathy as he followed Lyn down the corridor like a little boy about to be put into detention.

"He seemed a bit disorganised, don't you think?"

"Don't be taken in by the act. Dicky Summers is one of the brightest young teachers I've got. The kids love him, and his little antics keep their attention."

After a short walk, the pair passed through a solid-looking door adjacent to the front entrance of the school to be met by the pained expression of Tina Broughton, Lyn's secretary.

"Sorry, Lyn, it's the Cummings. They're in your office. I couldn't stop them."

Lyn winced.

"Not again? What's it about this time?"

Ant watched as Tina handed Lyn a note. Her reaction said it all.

"They're saying Tim's spelling isn't coming on quick enough."

Ant glanced at the note.

"It's not just their son's spelling that needs attention," chipped in Ant before watching Lyn fold the scrap of paper and slip it into her jacket pocket.

Lyn noticed Tina giving Ant the once-over.

"It's Anthony Stanton, isn't it?"

"Correct," replied Ant. "But—"

"Never forget a face, no matter how much age changes it," interrupted Tina without the slightest hint of sarcasm.

Ant's mouth remained half-open from his unfinished sentence as he tried to recall the woman.

"I was a dinner lady here when you two were kids. Always getting into trouble, I recall."

Lyn laughed; Ant blushed. Tina nodded her head towards Lyn's office.

"The sooner you're in, the sooner it'll be over, Lyn. I'll have a mug of strong coffee waiting for you."

Lyn let out a quiet moan before turning to Ant.

"Sorry. Looks like we're not going to get time to talk things over. Catch up with you later?"

"Don't apologise; I'm glad to escape. I'll use the time to ask around about Narky and catch up with you tonight. Don't forget, you're dining with us tonight. Mum and Dad can't wait to get us together!"

Lyn had already disappeared before he'd finished speaking.

"Don't worry. I'll remind her," said Tina as she showed Ant out of her office with a gentle pat to the small of his back. As he made his way to the exit, Tina called after him in a quiet voice.

"Be careful, Anthony. Narky has... mean had, some nasty

mates. It they think you're after them, they won't wait for you to knock on their door."

Ant noticed Tina nod in a conspiratorial fashion as if to emphasise her point.

Hmm, this chap gets more sinister by the day, thought Ant.

"I WILL NOT TELL you again, Lord Stanton. Keep out of my investigation, or I'll arrest you—and the schoolteacher."

The Wherry Arms fell silent as the detective let fly at Ant.

Unconcerned with the verbal assault, Ant turned from the bar to face his tormentor.

My dear Riley, you really do need to calm down. If you take blood pressure tablets, they don't seem to be working. Your cheeks are quite flushed."

A quiet laughter filled the small space as the locals enjoyed the spectacle.

Nothing better than winding up plod, especially this one, thought Ant as he took a sip of his drink and placed the pint glass carefully back on its beer mat.

"The thing is, Riley, I have an obligation to those who use my land, and..."

"And I'm telling you that owning a bit of land and having a fancy title doesn't entitle you to compromise a police investigation."

Ant's expression didn't change as the detective attempted to belittle him.

"I'd hardly call owning five thousand acres a bit of land, Detective, and as I told you previously, I couldn't have known the man was dead until I physically checked. I really do think I acted reasonably, don't you?"

The cackle of laughter from their engrossed audience continued with each exchange.

"Interfering with police evidence is a serious offence, Stanton. I won't tolerate it. Do you understand me?"

Ant took a second sip of his beer, winking at the barman as he lifted his glass.

"My dear detective—"

Ant's point was cut short by one of the barmaids handing over a phone that had been ringing for the last few seconds.

"It's for you."

Riley fumed as he waited for Ant to continue.

"Are you free? Where are you? Thank the Lord the morning's over. Now, where did you say you were?"

Ant held lazily on to the receiver as he watched the detective turn puce in the face before replying.

"I didn't, and well, I'm sort of free."

"What on earth's the matter with you? You're talking in riddles. Are you in the pub?"

"Yes."

It took Lyn two minutes to walk from the school to the village centre.

"Let me tell you one last time. I don't care if it's your land. And the same goes for your young lady. Leave it alone," barked Riley as he strode out of the bar, brushing past Lyn as she entered.

Lyn looked at Ant with bemusement as a round of applause broke out around them.

"Let's just say the dear inspector would rather we minded our own business. Not that he's getting anywhere, judging by his mood."

"Would you like another drink? And the young lady?" quipped the barman.

"Don't you start, Jed," replied Lyn. "Young lady, indeed."

She looked at Ant for his reaction before quickly looking away as Ant made eye contact.

Soon, the bar had returned to its normal gaggle of disparate conversations. Meanwhile, Lyn had seated herself next to Ant and placed her shoulder bag on the floor.

"I'm guessing it's not the usual," shouted Jed. You know, since you're at work and all that."

"Better just be a shandy, then, Jed," said Ant as he smiled at Lyn.

He could see she wasn't impressed.

"What," said Lyn as she glared at Ant. "Single lady likes to drink in a village pub?"

Ant smiled, savouring Lyn's flaring nostrils.

"Oh, shut up and just drink your beer."

The more Lyn bristled, the more Ant enjoyed the moment.

Ant hesitated just as he tasted the first of his new pint. Returning the glass to the table, Ant stared at its contents, transfixed by the amber liquid.

'Have you missed Fen Bodger pale ale so much you need to check it's still there?" said Lyn in a quizzical tone.

She was pleased to no longer be the source of his amusement.

"Jed," Ant shouted as he looked towards the barman. "Was Narky Collins a beer man or a shorts man?"

Ant could see Jed didn't need to think on the matter as he dried a glass with a towel that had seen better days.

"Too tight for shorts, that one. Guzzled beer like the rest of the lads."

Lyn caught on straight away.

"Interesting, that's what Glen's wife said," commented Ant.

As they digested the implications of Jed's response, Professor Pullman made his way over to the bar.

"I'll have a large bottle of your finest to take out, my man. Glen Stuart if you have it."

Jed's face beamed as he relished the sale of his most expensive whisky.

As Ant watched on, he was tapped on the shoulder from behind. He turned to see a familiar face.

"Hi, Alan. How're things with the history group. Found any more bodies recently?"

He watched Alan smile as the man entered into the spirit of things.

"Funny enough, we... Actually, no. But you never know, do you? Anyway, how are your investigations going?"

Ant smiled back at Alan then blinked an eye at Lyn.

"Funnily enough, things are beginning to get rather interesting."

LYN'S THOUGHTS wavered between the humdrum of her busy day at school and the confused matter of Narky Collins as she strolled the mile from home to Stanton Hall. Lyn knew Ant's parents were always pleased to see her. It was as if she provided a tangible link to Ant when he was away on active duty.

Turning a corner on the roadway with deep ditches on either side, so typical of rural Norfolk, Lyn smiled as the Hall came into sight, its clever landscaping hiding it from view until the last minute. Built in the fifteenth century, the profile of the building was a mixture of medieval, half-timbered façades, and later Georgian stonework with symmetrical windows.

What she hadn't expected to come across was a young woman sitting against a tree, staring at a mobile phone. As Lyn closed the distance between them, she heard a quiet whimper as the girl wiped tears from her cheek.

'It's Wendy, isn't it?" asked Lyn. She spoke in a soft, soothing tone calculated not to alarm the young woman.

The girl shifted her gaze from the phone to Lyn.

"Yes, but how do you know my name?"

"Oh, don't mind me. I'm a teacher, and it's a trick we learn along the way. You must have heard of word association?"

Lyn's question seemed to snap the girl out of her misery. Meeting Lyn's eyes, she settled back against the trunk of the magnificent oak.

"Suppose I have, but—"

"You're one of the professor's undergraduates up at the dig, aren't you?" interrupted Lyn. "You were talking to one of your colleagues when I passed the other day."

Lyn smiled as she spoke. It proved to be momentarily infectious.

"Oh yes, I see," replied Wendy before all trace of her grin disappeared.

By now, Lyn had reached the girl and perched next to her on the steep bank in which the giant tree stood.

"Want to talk?" asked Lyn as she put a comforting arm around the girl's shoulders.

Eventually the girl responded.

"He had a go at me for being late."

"Who did?" replied Lyn, "Your boyfriend?"

"No, no. The professor. But he told us the wrong time. He's always doing it. He's so disorganised. Then he blames us." Tears fell as she spoke.

Lyn summoned up all her years of teaching to put the girl at ease.

"Well, it's not the end of the world. From what I hear, that professor of yours seems to shout at everyone. Try not to take it so personally, and you'll be okay."

Lyn's words had little effect on Wendy.

"Now he won't answer his mobile." Her sobs became louder.

"Who, the professor?" replied Lyn, knowing her intervention was inadequate.

Wendy shoved the phone into her pocket before freeing herself of the tree.

"No, no, my boyfriend. Oh, you don't understand. It doesn't matter. I need to go."

Before Lyn could utter another word, Wendy walked away and rounded the corner, disappearing from her line of sight towards the village without saying another word.

"THAT WAS A LOVELY MEAL. Thank you, Gerald." Lyn's fulsome thanks to Ant's father for supper were genuine. She'd had a soft spot for the Earl and Countess of Stanton all her life. They'd offered a friendly space as a young teenager when her parents were arguing and she'd had enough.

"Brings us a cake every week, you know, Anthony. Chocolate's my favourite, isn't it, my dear?" The earl looked at Lyn then to his wife to whom he gave the gentlest of touches to the side of her cheek. Her eyes lit up as she smiled at her husband.

Ant had heard this story, like all the others many times,

as had Lyn. Both smiled and paid attention as if hearing it for the first time.

Lyn sensed her host's sudden change of mood.

"We've told Anthony he mustn't come back on our behalf. We know he's doing important hush-hush work. Isn't that right, my dear?"

Lady Stanton nodded, displaying a fragility that shocked Lyn.

She glimpsed at Ant and could see he looked uncomfortable at the sight of his elderly mother.

Thirty minutes passed until Ant's parents decided it was time for bed. Lyn waited patiently, and Ant spent a further ten minutes to check they were safely in bed.

"What do they say, Lyn? Once an adult, twice a child. God help us all; that's all I can say."

He shrugged his shoulders as he picked up an After Eight mint.

Lyn changed tack by telling him about the girl she'd met earlier.

"Then just as I thought she was talking about the professor, she cut me off and said 'boyfriend.' Strange, don't you think?"

Ant smiled and wagged a finger at his companion.

"Our little investigation is making you jump at shadows. Think about it. Young woman is upset and in her own world. Young woman is confronted by nosy stranger. Young woman does a runner. Hardly puts our dear professor in the firing line for murder most foul, does it?"

Lyn scowled at Ant, certain he wasn't taking her seriously.

"Stop it. You know what I mean. If you don't want me to help in this case, just say so."

She watched Ant's face drop but was in no mood to let him off the hook.

Ant opened his right hand and patted his chest with an open palm.

"Mea culpa, mea culpa—my fault."

Lyn raised her eyebrows.

"I know what the Latin stands for. It's not just for public-school boys and the Mafia, you know."

Lyn watched Ant frown as she made a rare reference to his teenage years at Eaton. She knew her comments had hit home and regretted the reference immediately.

"I'm sorry, Ant, I..."

"It's okay, Lyn. I was out of order. It's just that boyfriend/girlfriend stuff is a crazy thing to understand."

Lyn's eyes flashed at Ant as she suddenly felt uncomfortable.

Stupid man, she thought.

"Let's just say she did mean her boyfriend. She probably meant he had done the dirty on her or stood her up. That's all I'm saying. I tell you what. Why don't we track him down and see where it leads us—if you can get that Wendy girl to dish the dirt."

Lyn gave a slight nod of her head as she stood up, extended a hand, and brushed Ant's shoulder.

"It's getting late. Let's see what happens, eh?"

She crossed the spacious sitting room and opened the wide panelled door. Looking back at Ant, she could see he was lost in his own thoughts.

Perhaps we pushed each other too far tonight, she thought.

11

MORNING ASSEMBLY

Tuesday morning started like any other at Stanton Primary. Lyn, in her office working through the post, which as usual, Tina had opened and laid out in four neat piles:

Urgent

Can do later

For reading

File in bin

Lost in her thoughts about the previous evening, Lyn didn't hear the secretary enter.

"Best get going now, or you'll be late for morning assembly." The secretary was pointing at the clock on the wall in front of Lyn.

"Hell's bells," replied Lyn. "Nine o'clock already."

Lyn shot past a smiling Tina and took the twenty yards to the hall at a canter.

As she entered the room, the excited chatter of 200 five-to-ten-year-olds subsided as they caught sight of the head teacher.

All was in order. Children seated on the floor, legs and

arms crossed, their teachers and classroom assistants lining the side walls. Front and centre stood a wooden lectern, the day's prompt sheet having already been put in place, courtesy of Tina.

Twenty minutes later, Lyn was heading back to her office to begin the day's work.

"Coffee, yes, please," said Lyn as she re-entered her office and sat down opposite her secretary to go through her diary for the day.

"You say it every day as if it's the first time I've made you a coffee," replied Tina. She smiled as she gave her boss the gentle reproach.

"After keeping two hundred kids amused for twenty minutes, it feels like every day is the first time I've tasted coffee," Lyn joked.

The two women spent the next ten minutes exchanging gossip and confirming the running order for the day. This day would be like most other days: full, varied, but always challenging. It was just how Lyn liked it.

"Oh, by the way, those metal detectorists have confirmed they'll do the demonstration you asked for, tomorrow afternoon. I've phoned the professor, and although he's not happy about it, he's agreed they can use a strip of land just outside where he's been digging."

Lyn smiled.

"Heavens, they were quick. I didn't think for a moment they'd agree to it. Okay, tell the class teachers of those on this list it's a go, and let's make sure we get parental permission."

"Will do," replied Tina.

Alone in her office, Lyn again reflected on how Monday evening had ended.

I shouldn't have bitten like that, but he drives me nuts sometimes.

Lyn picked up the telephone receiver and dialled a familiar number.

Damn, that stupid answer machine, she thought. *Bet he's out and about cracking on with our investigation while I'm stuck here with loads of pointless paperwork and dealing with wonks from the county council.*

ANT WAS ENJOYING his morning driving around the estate on his quad bike. The endless landscape of the Norfolk Fens never ceased to amaze him.

He stopped for a moment to enjoy the sight of a kingfisher as it surveyed Stanton Broad from its favourite perch.

Now and then it would take to the skies then plunge into the Broad making hardly a ripple on its surface. Sometimes the bird would resurface empty mouthed. More often than not, its efforts were successful.

Ant's thoughts drifted to what he had been missing all these years. His joy was tempered with the responsibilities he knew went with coming back permanently.

Soon will be time to decide, he thought as he revved the quad's engine and made off towards a figure in the far distance.

"Thought it was you, Glen. Never-ending job mending the fences, I suppose."

The estate carpenter dropped his claw hammer to the grass and wiped a bead of sweat from his brow.

"You can say that again. Thousands of acres and open access for the public to most of it. Keeps me in a job, that's for sure."

A brief silence fell, and Ant sensed Glen wanted to say something but was hesitating. He guessed what it might be.

"How's your dad coming along, Glen?"

Ant's question helped the carpenter overcome his embarrassment.

"He's doing all right, Mr Anthon... er, Ant. That is, except for having the laptop taken off him. I've told him, no more bingo, that's for sure."

Ant smiled, which was the signal for Glen to give himself permission to laugh.

"He wasn't pleased at first, mind you. But the threat of the bailiffs lifting his prized Welsh dresser did the trick."

"Talking about bailiffs, Glen, is everything okay on that front?"

Glen nodded.

"That's all sorted. I can't thank you enough, Ant."

Ant nodded, reaching over and patting Glen by way of reassurance.

"Got to look after each other. Isn't that right, Glen?"

"All the same, thank you. I won't forget it."

Ant raised a hand and pointed towards the dig site.

"Talking about not forgetting, something I meant to ask you yesterday. I'm trying to track Narky's movements in the days running up to his death. You didn't say when you last saw him, Glen."

Ant watched Glen's reaction carefully. The carpenter's cheek betrayed the slightest of twitches as he formulated his response.

"Oh, er, sometime early last week, I think."

Ant didn't push the matter any further but took note of Glen's hesitant response.

I hope Glen's telling me the truth, thought Ant and made a mental note to check out his story.

"That's great, Glen. I just want to get things clear in my head. Now I must be off. Best of luck with the fence."

Revving the engine with a flick of his right wrist he turned the machine and roared off into the distance not waiting for the carpenter to respond.

12

FIELD SURFING

"Love this time of evening, don't you, Lyn?" said Ant as he let loose the final mooring rope of his father's boat, *Field Surfer.*

Lyn nodded her agreement and took in the lazy sunshine of a quiet Tuesday evening.

Free from its ties, the vintage vessel glided away from its mooring as Ant jumped aboard and allowed the craft to drift into the middle of the Broad.

Ant busied himself setting the wherry's distinctive triangular sail.

"Take the tiller, will you?"

Lyn did as Ant asked, practising a skill she'd used many times before on their outings on the wherry.

"Now that we have some peace and quiet, shall we go over our investigation? I'm worried that Riley will get to the murderer first, and that wouldn't do at all."

Ant finished tying off the rigging and deftly walked towards the stern.

"I'd forgotten how competitive you are, Lyn."

She eased the tiller to the left and guided *Field*surfer around a gentle bend in Stanton Broad.

"But you're right; if we don't crack on, that stupid policeman will beat us to it. That said, from what I'm hearing around the village, he's still treating the death as if it were accidental."

Lyn shook her head.

"He may have had a go at you in the Wherry Arms, but if he thinks that, he hasn't spoken to Jed, has he?"

Ant nodded, indicating he agreed.

"Lyn, if there's one thing I know about our dear constabulary, it's that once the investigating officer gets an idea into their head, the whole team runs with it; they've no choice. Riley is convinced Narky fell into that trench in a drunken stew and poleaxed himself when he landed."

Ant warmed to his theme.

"Let's take a step back and look at what we know about Narky. He was a bully and thirsty for cash. Perhaps Glen wasn t the only one he was trying to screw for money."

Lyn gently pushed the tiller to her right to keep *Field Surfer* in the centre of the Broad.

"Without knowing what he had against other men in the village, we could be looking at dozens of suspects, none of whom we could put under suspicion until we'd have spoken to them. After all, what did any of them have that needed a favour from a brute like Narky? It's just not a logical avenue for us to go down, Ant."

He detected the spark of inspiration from Lyn as she finished speaking.

"Yes?" said Ant.

"Wait a minute. What about... the professor?"

He smiled and gave a single clap of his hands.

"Spot on, Lyn. Think about it: the prof needed access to

the land, and Narky controlled that. Perhaps, as the dig produced more finds, the professor wanted extra time, and Narky threatened to close the site down if he didn't pay up?"

"And we've seen how short tempered the professor is when he doesn't get his own way, and we also know he's a whisky drinker."

"Right again, Lyn."

Ant could see from Lyn's expression that she had enjoyed the compliment and acknowledgement of her contribution to the investigation.

Got to make more effort on that front, he thought.

Lyn pointed towards the unfolding landscape ahead.

"You know, it still gives me a thrill every time I'm on the Broads. There's something about the calmness and space that gets to me."

Ant smiled as he recalled their adventures on *Field Surfer* as children.

"What, even when Dad was barking orders and moaning about us mucking up his prized mahogany decking with blackcurrant juice and the like?"

Lyn laughed.

"It certainly was the love of his life, wasn't it?" Lyn replied. "He spent years renovating her. Oh, and by the way, you were the mucky one, if I remember."

Ant returned Lyn's smile as he watched the boat slide effortlessly along the water making full use of the following breeze.

He scanned the horizon as the Broad opened out into a wide basin, its banks obscured by swaying stands of Norfolk reed. Overhead, set against the reddening sky and setting sun, a heron patrolled its territory on the lookout for an opportunistic meal.

"Just to confuse things, what if Narky was bumped off by

that girl you came across last night—or at least someone she knew? After all, what was she doing by the Hall at that time of night?"

Ant's sudden switch back to their investigation caught Lyn by surprise.

'What do you mean?"

"Well, think about it. Perhaps whoever killed Narky thought we were getting too close; what better way to find out what we're up to than keep watch on us?"

Lyn shook her head in disbelief.

"Isn't the idea of covert surveillance that you hide, not stand by a tree on a quiet country road wailing your eyes out?'

Ant thought for a moment and allowed his hand to brush the water, his fingers causing a tiny ripple in its surface.

"Hmm, I think what you are saying to me is that I've lost the plot."

He noticed a look of irony spreading across her face.

"To paraphrase your good self: got it in one."

The point wasn't lost on Ant. He changed the subject.

"You know, being stuck on the A47 from time to time makes me think that moving freight by water again might not be such a bad idea."

Lyn protested.

"What, and spoil all this?"

"Can't be any worse than summer tourists in their hire boats causing havoc and almost decapitating themselves on our low bridges, can it?"

The banter tailed off into silence as the wherry continued its sedate progress.

Two glasses of white wine later and a dimming light

indicated it was time to turn the wherry through 360 degrees and make for home.

"Watch out for the boom, Lyn."

She pulled the tiller hard and watched the sail flick from port to starboard. Having learnt from bitter experience, Lyn ducked allowing the boom to swing from one side of the boat to the other without hindrance.

"And before you say anything, my trusty deckhand, it wasn't my fault you fell in when we were nine."

Lyn signalled her disagreement.

"I beg to differ. You told me to fetch you the rope, knowing I'd have to stand up just before you tacked. Even your dad said it was your fault."

Lyn's concocted glare defied Ant to argue the case.

He still tried.

"As a matter of fact, I remember Dad saying it was just as much your fault for being daft enough to fall for my little jape."

"Ha ha. You admit it. You were to blame!"

Irritated at being manipulated into an admission of guilt, Ant gave the boom a push causing the wherry to jink to the left. This time Lyn was ready.

"I'm not nine anymore, Admiral Nelson."

Ant watched as a wry smile crossed her lips as she corrected the tiller to counteract Ant's attempt to catch her out.

As the vessel neared its mooring, the land sloped upward. On the horizon, the outline of dig site tents stood out against the fading sun.

"Here, grab this and tie her off," said Ant as he threw a hemp rope in Lyn's general direction.

As the familiar sight of the village green came into view, the pair veered to the left and made for the pond. They leant against a rusted rail and watched the ducks gather expectantly in front of them.

"What about your carpenter? Could he have anything to do with it?"

As she spoke, she fidgeted in her pocket for remnants she'd fed the throng with earlier in the day.

'I want to believe he's innocent, but there's something nagging at me that I need to get to the bottom of."

"Worried your loyalty to a long-standing tenant family is getting in the way of your objectivity?"

Ant turned to look at Lyn.

"Something like that."

The pair broke off eye contact to watch half a dozen ducks scurry for the crumbs on offer.

The conversation fell quiet again. The lights of the Wherry Arms flickered across the village pond. Familiar sights and sounds of a full pub filled the air. The only other noise involved Phyllis berating Betty on village gossip as they scurried home from the shop. From what Ant could deduce, Betty continued to survive their friendship only by taking every opportunity to agree with whatever it was Phyllis was saying.

Ant pulled away from the railings and pointed towards the pub.

"Your round, yes?"

"Not so fast, matey. We need to agree what we do next. Your pale ale can wait."

Lyn's rebuke made Ant focus.

"Okay, I'll catch up with the professor tomorrow then check out Glen's alibi. Now, time for that drink. Remember, you're paying."

Ant was across the narrow road and through the door of the pub before Lyn had much chance to respond.

13

A GOLDEN AFTERNOON

"Well, you did the landlord's takings a power of good when you bought that whisky," said Ant as he ambled across to Professor Pullman.

The academic didn't acknowledge Ant at first; instead, he concentrated on zipping the entrance to his tent shut.

Ant watched as Pullman slowly turned in the general direction of his voice.

"Ah, yes, Mr... or is it Lord... Stanton. Never got the hierarchy of the English nobility into my head, I'm afraid." Pullman let out a brief, nervous laugh.

Ant studied the professor as the trace of a snigger spread across the man's face.

Not impressed, matey, thought Ant.

"A little surprising, Professor, given you live in the past, so to speak?"

Ant didn't give Pullman an opportunity to respond. Instead, he watched his cheeks flush and eyes narrow.

"Given my father is the Earl of Stanton, as his eldest surviving son, it accords me the courtesy title of Lord, though actually, if we're being precise, as I know you like to be, our family name is Norton-D'Arcy, so if you wish to be formal about it, you may address me as Lord Anthony Norton-D'Arcy of Stanton."

Ant was enjoying goading the academic and could see from the man's pursed lips how well his remarks had hit home.

"But let's not stand on ceremony, Professor. We are all friends here, aren't we?"

Ant's upward inflection at the end of his comment, together with deliberate pause, invited a response from the professor. Once again, Ant didn't give him a chance to respond.

"Listen, why don't you call me Anthony. We're not ones for standing on ceremony around here, at least not amongst friends." Ant knew he had put the professor back in his box and exposed the academic's befuddled routine.

Professor Pullman turned from Ant to check the tent zip for a second time.

Ant knew the man was playing for time.

"Yes, yes, quite right, er, Anthony."

His efforts to distract attention from his stupidity didn't divert Ant's unblinking stare. Point made, Ant took the temperature out of their dialogue, if for no other reason than he wanted something important from Pullman. Information.

Not yet the time to press home my advance, thought Ant.

"Glen Stuart is a favourite whisky of mine too."

Ant could see that his change in tone had thrown the professor.

"Oh, I see. Is it?"

"It is, Professor. Scotland's finest. Though not cheap, as you know. But well worth the price."

Ant watched as the professor's demeanour changed. Suddenly he looked nervous.

"As I was saying, Professor."

"What, yes, indeed. The landlord at the Wherry Arms was, as you say, most grateful for the sale. And please forgive me for not saying hello in the pub, by the way, but the detective inspector seemed rather keen to speak with you."

The professor pulled himself to his full height and relapsed into his more usual cocky tone.

The man's renewed confidence didn't impress Ant. From memory, he recalled that by the time the professor was at the bar buying whisky, Inspector Riley had left.

"It was an emergency," continued the professor. "You see, I was replacing a bottle stolen from my tent."

Pullman half turned and nodded towards his accommodation.

Ant's eyes followed, his brain racing to make sense of the professor's unexpected response.

He could see that the man was studying him closely and worked hard not to show any reaction to the professor's explanation.

"Always happy to help our wonderful police force," replied Ant, trying to throw Pullman off balance. "They asked about my drinking habits. I imagine they've asked you too?"

Ant watched the professor for signs of agitation. There were none.

"No, no. In fact, I've seen little of the police. Not since that terrible day. Why should they be interested in an elderly academic's habits?"

It was Ant's turn to think on his feet.

Slippery fish, this one, thought Ant.

"Oh, no reason, or at least none they mentioned to me. You know the police. Information is power and all that."

The professor shrugged his shoulders.

"Glad to say I have little to do with the police. Not much call for them on archaeological digs... unless we find human remains less than two hundred years old, that is."

Ant allowed the professor to play his little game.

"And until the discovery of that unfortunate man, I had seen neither hide nor hair of the police."

As the pair took measure of the other, Ant broke his eye contact to survey the dig site. An area of around five acres, he could see the land was punctuated with several slit trenches and spoil heaps. To one side stood a large temporary building where, from its open entrance he could see, all artefacts came for cleaning before being catalogued. Next to this stood a cluster of smaller tents Ant guessed housed the undergraduates and other academics involved in the project.

"So has it been worthwhile?"

The professor hesitated.

"In the main, yes. We knew an extensive villa complex existed here. And as expected, we discovered a hypocaust used for the underfloor heating to the complex. A bonus was the smaller buildings. Servants' quarters, we think."

Ant nodded then pointed to two trenches that joined at right angles.

"Why excavate like that?"

"Well, we had a hunch that the complex met a violent end, and we've found evidence of burning. Given the owners were clearly of high status and wealthy, we were surprised not to find any precious metals."

"Perhaps they left in a hurry. You know, if they were being attacked or something?"

Ant watched as the professor gesticulated with his hands pointing first at one part of the excavation then another.

That's got him going, thought Ant.

"Yes, we think an attack by Boudica. But that's the point, you see. In such circumstances, precious items are often buried in haste. The theory is that owners hoped to retrieve them at a later date. But here, nothing. Also... what the... Blast."

The professor's words trailed off as he spotted a group of people on the far side of the dig site.

"Problem, Professor?"

"You might say so. That silly school asked if they could bring a group of children up here so that irritating metal-detecting group can show them how their infernal machines work."

Ant could see the academic fizz as he watched the gaggle of excited children form a circle around half a dozen adults. Pullman marched towards the group, his hands waving in all directions.

"Not too close. I told that woman. Only on that side of the tape, if you please. Don't you understand English?"

Ant smiled as he followed the academic, soon spotting Lyn at the centre of the group. As usual, she was directing operations, which he acknowledged was no small task when dealing with excited youngsters.

Ducking under the red-and-white, plastic tape that indicated the dig boundary, Ant came within listening distance of Lyn's group. He could see four detectorists demonstrating their machines and explaining what the different tones meant. Meanwhile, Lyn and her secretary circled the children like a pair of sheepdogs, watching out for stragglers.

The professor stood, arms folded, eyes peeled for any incursion onto his precious dig site.

'Children, who wants to have a go at finding treasure?"

Ant recoiled from the volume and pitch of screams coming from the children. They volunteered as a pack.

Hell's bells, I've known quieter battlefields, thought Ant.

"Settle down," said Lyn in a calm, assertive voice. "Everyone will get their chance. Now, James, Carol, Nick, Chloe. You four first."

The youngsters stepped forward, brimming with pride at being, in their eyes, first amongst equals. The rest let out a collective moan.

Ant watched as the professionals explained how to work a metal detector. He also noted that the professor intensified his gaze, watching for any infringement of his agreement with Lyn.

"His voice doesn't half grind," said Ant as he joined Lyn watching the excited youngsters.

"He does shout rather a lot, doesn't he, and so disorganised. Apparently, he's always forgetting stuff. At least that's what the undergraduate said I came across. You know, the one—"

"Yes, yes."

He had no wish to be reminded a second time he'd not been listening when Lyn told him about the distressed girl. "Perhaps he's just your typical academic. Bright as a button without an ounce of common sense. Or perhaps that's what he'd like people to think?"

His train of thought was interrupted by yet another increase in noise from the children as a detector let out a bright, sharp sound. Ant watched the attention the signal got from the four professional detectorists. Silence descended as one of the detectorists helped a young student turn a clod of soil with a short spade.

"Found a hoard, have you?" asked Ant, a broad smile spreading across his cheeks.

As he spoke, the child got up from his knees and held something to the light. The artefact glinted in the sun.

A gold coin.

The professor attempted to snatch the coin from the child.

"You must all vacate the dig. This land is an important archaeological site, and its history must not be disturbed by amateurs."

An embarrassed silence descended. Ant filled the void.

"Professor, as you know, this is my family's land and not yours. I will decide who, and who does not, access it."

Ant watched as the professor wasted no time in protesting.

"An artefact of historical importance has emerged. I demand that—"

Ant had had enough.

"You demand nothing, Professor. Now, shall we all enjoy the find by having a good look at it, children?"

Pullman's chastened reply disappeared beneath a collective cheer from the children.

It took only a few minutes for the children to tire of examining the coin.

Might as well have been a bottle top, thought Ant, before noticing Lyn trying to catch his eye.

"Lyn, time to get this lot back to school before they scatter all over the place. Professor, I suppose you might want the coin?"

Ant could see Pullman didn't need asking twice. He

snatched the precious artefact and made off at pace for the finds tent.

That just left Ant and the four detectorists looking at the hole left from digging the coin up.

“That reminds me,” said Ant as he watched the detectorists pack away their beloved machines. “Can you ask Vikki to get in touch. I'd like to speak to her again. You’ve all been so good with the kids. The least I can do is buy her a new machine—but don't tell her why I want to see her.”

Ant immediately saw how pleased his offer went down with her colleagues.

As they were leaving, one of the group turned back to Ant.

“Funny thing is, it's not the first time that hole has been dug.”

Ant looked puzzled.

“What I mean is, whoever first dug that hole knew what they were doing. We have a special way of doing it, you see, so that when we put the loose earth back, we leave as little damage as possible. Farmers don’t like a mess being left that might hurt their beasts."

Ant nodded.

"I get what you mean; beasts with broken legs are not a pleasant sight."

The detectorists nodded in agreement.

“So you're saying that someone who knows what they are doing goes to the trouble of digging a great hole. And to cap it all, they leave a gold coin that a child manages to find?”

“That’s my point. I don’t think it was so much not finding it, rather leaving it behind. Perhaps they were in a hurry?” replied the detectorist.

Ant looked back at the hole.

"Are you saying there's more down there?"

"I'm saying it's likely there *was* more than one coin down there."

The detectorist held a shard of unglazed pottery in front of him.

Ant examined the fragment of baked clay.

"What is it?"

"We think it's part of the pot that contained a hoard. From its diameter of this bit, I'd say it was huge. Look, there are more remnants scattered around, so I'm sure we're right. We're just surprised the professor didn't pick up on it."

Ant's suspicions intensified.

A professor who plays the fool, a detectorist who claims she suffered an attack, and a would-be blackmailer.

Time to try out a few theories, thought Ant.

14

GIFT HORSES

"Wow, a great place you've got. Beats my studio flat," said Vikki as she strolled along the marble-columned entrance and into Stanton Hall's oak-panelled morning room.

Ant's eyes followed Vikki's gaze up to the high ceiling decorated with gilded plasterwork. At its centre hung a glittering crystal chandelier.

"An accident of history as it happens. Believe it or not, one of my ancestors won it on the turn of a card. Fortunately for the family, the guy died before his luck at cards ran out and he lost it again."

Vikki smiled, shaking her head in disbelief as he gave her a potted history of the Hall.

"And one thing the male line paid particular attention to was marrying well. Hence, we're still here."

"Not earned wealth, then?"

Ant looked at Vikki, his eyes narrowing in playful rapprochement.

"Do I detect the merest hint of disapproval? Perhaps

you're right, but we do our bit to use the estate to help the village economy."

Vikki laughed again.

"Yeah right, I bet you do."

Ant led his companion through to the great hall and into one corner. Behind an ornate Georgian sofa stood two old, red leather fire buckets, on which faded traces of the family coat of arms remained just visible.

"Alas, they're not needed in case of fire. The opposite, in fact. When it rains, we have these all over the Hall; it's one thing to own a grade-one-listed building. Quite another having the dosh to keep it going."

Ant was impressed as he watched Vikki look closer at the fabric of the building with what looked to him like a keen interest.

Perhaps she does understand, he thought.

On went the tour, room by room, until they arrived at the library.

"Dad's favourite room," said Ant as he made his way over to a large mahogany reading table on which rested an oblong box with a picture of a metal detector on the side.

"Here, for you."

Vikki's cheeks flushed.

"This is so generous of you... and I'm sorry if—"

"Not at all, it's a perfectly reasonable reaction. I thought much the same myself growing up here. That was until I realised how many villagers rely on the Hall for their living."

Ant sensed Vikki relaxing, which given the real reason for his invitation, he knew to be important.

"As for the detector. You deserve it. Your club has done so much for us, both on the dig, and in working with the kids."

Before either could continue with their conversation, a

quiet knock on the heavy oak doors interrupted their flow. In walked one of the day helpers with a tray of tea and shortcake biscuits.

"Great job, Tim. Thanks for that."

The immaculately dressed young man placed the refreshments on a side table next to an unlit fire.

Vikki had a "how did he do that" look on her face as Ant handed the perplexed woman her tea, courtesy of a delicate bone-china cup and saucer.

"Not magic, Vikki. I arranged for Tim to bring us drinks when he heard us enter the library. Milk and sugar? And how about a biscuit?"

Vikki declined the sugar and nabbed two biscuits as she accepted his invitation to sit.

Several minutes passed as they exchanged views on securing access to land by detectorists and the scourge of nighthawking.

Ant turned the conversation to more pressing matters.

"It certainly was a nasty business up at the dig site, wasn't it? I mean someone going for you like that. Then there's the dead bloke."

Once again, Ant watched Vikki's body language to see if his gentle probing had any giveaway signs of defensiveness.

Am I on the money, or is two and two making five? he thought.

He could see Vikki looked uncomfortable.

"Please, forgive me. I didn't mean to bring back memories of something I quite understand you'd rather forget."

"It's okay," said Vikki, her voice shaking. "You're right. It was horrible. But at least I'm still here. The one thing I can't get out of my head is what if..."

Vikki's voice tailed off as she gazed into the blackened fire at the back of the stone hearth.

Ant allowed the silence to continue until he judged she'd gathered her composure.

"Best not to think about the 'what ifs.' You're here; you're safe. That's what matters, Vikki."

Ant could see that his guest took comfort from his words.

Now or never, thought Ant.

"The thing is, Vikki, the killer is still out there, and you can help catch whoever murdered Narky."

Vikki's eyes began to veer away from the hearth and towards Ant. Her hands gripped the lionhead armrests of her chair.

"How? I've already told you everything. I was up there with permission. A man jumped me. I walloped him and ran—and I didn't see a body."

He watched as her eyes burned into him. Her tone exuded defiance.

Ant nodded his head as she spoke. His intention was to show empathy.

"Something is nagging away at me. A conundrum, you might say."

Ant headed off Lyn's attempt to divert his line of questioning.

He continued.

"I don't believe someone as committed to metal detecting as you, having paid almost two thousand pounds for your machine, would just leave it where you dropped it."

Ant allowed the silence to do its work.

"What do you mean? I told you I killed no one. I didn't know a man had died until your friend told me, so—"

"But that's my point," Ant interrupted. "I accept you were not involved. And so you had no reason to believe the man who attacked you would still be there later that night."

Vikki broke off eye contact. Her head dropped. She slumped into the safety of the thick leather, button-back chair.

"So you see. If I had been you, I'd have gone back to collect my metal detector. That's what you did, wasn't it, Vikki?"

She half turned her head to look at her interrogator.

He sensed the words she wanted to say wouldn't come.

She nodded her head.

Ant raised himself from the chair and crossed the few feet that separated them. He crouched beside the woman and took hold of her hand. His reassurance worked as he felt her white-knuckle grip on the chair arm loosen.

"I went back on Friday evening. Like you said, I assumed no one would be up there, and I wanted my detector back. But as I got to the top of the slope, I could hear two voices. Two men arguing."

"Yes, go on," interrupted Ant in a low, quiet voice.

"They didn't see me... and I sure as hell didn't want to get involved. I assumed they were nighthawks. You know, like I explained before, detectorists that dig land when it's dark without permission and steal whatever they find."

"But why?" he asked, his voice quiet and non-judgemental.

Vikki grimaced.

"Bad lot, they are. We all get tarred with the same brush."

Ant could see, almost feel, the depth of her hatred she felt for such people.

"I get you. But let me ask again. Why did you think they were detecting?"

"Because the fat one was on his knees digging at something. The other one, the thin one, was standing over him shouting his head off."

Ant could see the effect the recollection was having on Vikki.

"I know it's hard, but can you remember what the thin bloke said?"

Vikki's eyes scanned the books lining the surrounding shelves as if she were searching for the words to use.

"Look. While they were arguing I saw my detector, grabbed it, and ran like hell before they cottoned on I was there."

She pulled her hand away from Ant's reassuring embrace as if to confirm the interrogation was over and she intended to leave.

Ant sensed he had only one more chance to prise further information from her.

"Listen. I know you had nothing to do with Narky's murder. Do you hear me? You have done nothing wrong. But if there's anything more you can remember about that night, it might just help catch the killer."

By now he had clasped Vikki's hand again. His voice deep and quiet. His eyes not allowing Vikki to break eye contact.

She closed her eyes as if running a film tape, turning her head like a downhill skier practising the twists and turns of the course before leaving the starting gate.

"'Leave it. Leave it down there.' That's what the thin one said... or something like that. Yes, I'm sure that's what he said. At least that's all I heard."

Ant worked hard to hide his excitement.

Now we're cooking with gas, he thought.

"Vikki, you've been so brave. Thank you. Who knows,

you might just have helped clear this mess up and get a killer off the streets."

IMPATIENT TO TELL Lyn about his evening's work, Ant picked up the 1970s-style phone at the bottom of the hall staircase and dialled her number. Frustrated at not getting an answer he left a breathy message.

15

ABSENT FRIENDS

"At least you picked my message up this time," said Ant as Lyn shut the front door, and he followed her into the kitchen. "I thought you didn't like mess."

Lyn shrugged her shoulders as she looked upon the scene of general dishevelment with heaps of student exercise books scattered around the worktops.

"This is the result of just one member of staff going off sick. Dozens of the stupid things to mark, and a Rubik's Cube of a puzzle to redo the staff timetables."

Ant headed over to the coffee percolator and grabbed two mugs.

"Then I guess you could do with one of these?"

As Ant handed Lyn the steaming drink, he folded the timetable planner in two with his free hand.

"Don't think you'd appreciate me spilling coffee all over your new staff rotas."

Lyn didn't need to answer. Ant could see her look was enough.

"What's so important you needed to stop me working out how to cover my classes tomorrow?"

Ant could see she hadn't the slightest interest in his unexpected visit.

"You know. Narky's been dead for almost a week now, and the police, as far as I know, are nowhere near finding out how or why he ended up in that ditch. That's because..."

"That's because Riley thinks there's nothing to investigate."

Ant waited for Lyn to finish then left several seconds before continuing for added effect.

"That's because Riley's lazy and looking for a quick fix."

Lyn shook her head as she again focused on the piles of student work awaiting attention.

Ant followed his friend's eyes around the room.

"What if I told you Vikki King holds the key to this whole thing?"

Lyn's eyes flashed, her attention on Ant restored.

"Remember, it was you who thought she killed him all along, and—"

She interrupted again.

"And?"

Lyn placed her mug of coffee on the table.

"If you would let me finish," said Ant, his voice tinged with frustration at having his flow curtailed. "I have an idea how we can prove she did, or did not, do it."

Ant watched Lyn play with her mug, turning it on the spot by its handle.

"Well, Sherlock, what's your plan?"

Ant smiled. He'd known his friend long enough to know when he was being goaded.

"I refuse to rise to that," he said, acknowledging Lyn's smirk.

Ant explained his meeting with Vikki earlier in the day.

Lyn listened, examining every word to see if it reinforced her belief she'd been right about "VK."

"But that doesn't move us on much, does it? Yes, Vikki's admitted she went back for her detector and saw a thin bloke standing over a fat bloke digging. What if they were nighthawks after all? We'll never find them, let alone prove either had anything to do with Narky's death."

Ant once again made his way over to the coffee percolator and topped up both mugs before resuming his chair.

"There were no nighthawks up there that night." Ant spoke with a certainty that surprised Lyn.

"How can you be so sure?" The dig has been on regional TV several times, so plenty of people knew of its existence. Also, I'm told the detectorist club advertised the rally in at least four specialist magazines plus loads of detectorist forums. If I was inclined to do a spot of midnight treasure hunting, I'd have known where to be. After all, I'd be one of a hundred comparative strangers roaming the place swinging a detector."

Ant nodded, acknowledging the logic of Lyn's argument.

"I know because I checked," replied Ant. "In fact, there has been no nighthawk activity in this part of Norfolk for six months. Not since the police nabbed three blokes in April near Wells-next-the-Sea. They won't be out of prison for a year or two yet."

Lyn held her coffee midway between the table and her lips, waving a plume of steam away from her face.

"Checked? I thought you couldn't stand the police?"

Ant risked overacting as he folded his arms and elevated his chin.

"That's a terrible impression of Mussolini. And that didn't end well for him, did it?" chided Lyn.

Ant's hurt look amused Lyn. His pride pricked, he resumed without the folded arms or puffed-out chest.

"Intelligence work comes with its perks, Lyn. I do not need to trouble the likes of our beloved Riley when I need information, if you get my drift."

"Don't be so pompous, Ant. It doesn't suit you," quipped Lyn, determined to ground her best friend.

It was Ant's turn to play with his coffee mug now.

"Anyway, you were telling me about what Vikki said to you before she left. Come on, let's have it, Sherlock." Lyn spoke with a renewed interest, having bested her friend.

"Hmm," Ant replied, not at all pleased Lyn had won round one in the "who's the boss" stakes.

Deciding not to dwell on the verbal beating Lyn had given him, Ant erred on the side of brevity.

"Vikki told me the thin one said, 'Leave it down there.'"

Ant watched as Lyn thought for a moment and looked over to a pine plate rack hanging on the wall to her right, her eyes dancing as if she were counting its contents.

"What if the fat one was Narky, and he'd found something the thin one wanted?"

"Or he went to retrieve something the thin one had already discovered? And what if the thin one was the one who jumped her earlier that night?" said Ant.

Lyn jumped up to retrieve a scrap of paper from the sideboard in the hallway.

"I drew this last weekend when I was trying to make sense of what happened the night Narky was murdered."

She laid her sketch out on the tabletop.

"So here's the trench where Narky was found. And here's the spoil heap." Lyn's finger moved over the sketch at a feverish pace as she shared its contents. "Over here are the archaeologists' accommodation and the finds tent."

The only area not marked was where Vikki said she saw the two men arguing.

Ant filled in the missing information.

"It was here, given the position she must have been in as she came up the slope. This must be it."

He pointed to a position on Lyn's sketch then marked it with a pen taken from his breast pocket.

Both studied the document, moving fingers across its surface as they conjectured what might have happened.

"Hang on," said Lyn as she tapped a finger on the map. "That's around the position one of my pupils found the coin."

Ant noticed her eyes widen as the connection she'd made hit home.

He paced around the dining table without once taking his eyes off the sketch.

"So," he began, "let's assume the fat one was Narky Collins. We know he was hungry for money. To end up in a trench with his head caved in must mean he was trying to relieve someone else of a great deal of cash—"

"Or something worth a lot of money?" Lyn interrupted.

"Yes," replied Ant. "The question is, who was he stealing from?"

He could see Lyn was deep in thought, her eyes fixed on the sketch.

"Lyn?"

"I wonder," she said.

Ant decided not to ask the obvious question; instead, letting his friend follow through in her own time.

"You know the girl I mentioned to you. The one I came across when—"

"Her again? Wendy, wasn't it?"

"Well, I spotted her going into Hammond's Bakery at

lunchtime when I was travelling back to school from a meeting. Turns out she bought a tuna bap. Not my cup of tea, but..."

Ant couldn't hide his exasperation at the needless detail.

Lyn ignored his protest.

"So I took the opportunity to sit with her under the old buttercross and have a chat. She was a lot calmer than the other night, I can tell you. In fact, she apologised."

Ant frowned.

"And...?"

Lyn sighed.

"Well, it turns out someone wasn't where they should have been. With Wendy, I mean."

Ant understood at once.

"The question is, if they didn't meet Wendy, where were they last Friday night?"

"Got it in one," replied Lyn, her face mirroring Ant's in their growing anticipation at having cracked the case.

"I've got an idea," said Ant, as he leant into the table and pointed at a small circle on the sketch.

"Meet me here at ten tomorrow morning. And I need these people with you. All of them. I don't care what you tell them: just get them up there."

Ant scribbled several names on the back of Lyn's sketch before passing it to her.

"Good job I've a good deputy head. Friday can be a hell of a day at school, you know," said Lyn as she glanced at the list.

16

HATS OFF

Hope Lyn got everyone there, thought Ant as he ran through how he intended to unmask Narky's killer. He rehearsed what might go wrong. Above all, he didn't want to make a fool of himself in front of Detective Inspector Riley. Ant knew his pride shouldn't come into it. But...

Not going to happen, he thought.

"What's all this about, Anthony?" asked the professor, as he spotted his patron approaching.

Ant held his hand.

"Nice to see you, again, Professor. The place looks busy today," replied Ant, ignoring the academic's question.

Professor Pullman shook the hand, his grip firm.

"That head-teacher woman wishes to dragoon me into a meeting in the finds tent. She's already press-ganged a number of my staff. Said you wanted to talk to us all about something important?"

Ant could see Pullman's response laid bare his irritation at being told what to do. He played with the academic.

"Come, come, Professor. It sounds like you don't like being ordered around by a woman?"

He led Pullman to the finds tent, pleased that Pullman bit as he bristled at Ant's implied accusation of misogyny.

Ant deployed a well-trodden management trick, guaranteed to cement his position as top dog between the two.

"Don't be so defensive, Professor."

Pullman fell for it and gave Ant the response he'd anticipated.

"Defensive. I'm not, I—"

Ant purposely interrupted the professor.

"You are, Professor, but not to worry; we're here now."

Ant knew his tactic to be a cheap shot, but he knew its effect would be important in forcing the professor onto the back foot.

That worked a treat, thought Ant.

Ant pulled aside the entrance flap of the finds tent, which rippled in the strong breeze that had wafted across the dig site all morning.

"Please take a seat, Professor. Here, let me help you," said Ant as he cleared items of clothing from a vacant chair. He gestured for the academic to sit.

"Good morning, Detective Inspector Riley. Thank you for coming. Of course you know the professor. Not sure if you've met Glen Dawson, who is our estate carpenter, Also, Vikki King, a local metal detectorist?"

Ant pointed to the two individuals in turn.

"By the way, you two. Thank you for responding to Lyn's invitation so positively."

The police force's representative was less content with unfolding events.

"We passed the time of day while waiting for your gracious arrival," replied Riley.

"I suppose you think you're clever?"

Ant smiled as he watched Riley take out his pocketbook with an exaggerated flourish.

"Wasting police time is a serious offence, you know."

Ant purposely turned away from the detective before the man had finished speaking.

"Wasting your time is the last thing I wish to do, Riley."

Ant could see his ruse had worked as the policeman stiffened, clearly taking umbrage at his tormentor's attitude. Ant knew Riley was all the angrier for having to put up with treatment he'd accept from no one but his superiors.

Point made; Ant continued.

"It's about Narky Collins. Now I know that you, Detective Inspector, and your team have tried your hardest to solve the case, but—"

He could see Riley was spitting feathers to interrupt his nemesis.

"Solve *the case*? What do you mean, man? The matter is closed. That unfortunate man fell into the trench in a drunken stupor, hit his head, and died. That's an end to it; do you hear?"

Ant saw Riley looked self-satisfied putting his interrogator in his place. The three other guests also relaxed on hearing the detective's conclusions.

Ant pressed a finger to his lips, frowned, and tilted his head forward as if in deep thought.

"Well," said Ant, raising his head and looking towards Riley, "what if I told you how Mr. Collins *really* met his end? And what if I could prove murder and hand the killer over to you this morning?"

"What are you talking about, man? Are you mad? Proof? What proof?"

As Riley finished speaking, two figures entered the tent.

"Ah, Lyn, good to see you both. Simon, thank you for coming. Take a seat," said Ant.

The detective's confused state reached new heights as the pair occupied the two remaining chairs.

"And who may I ask is this young man?"

The detective gave Simon a withering stare.

"Oh, he's one of my undergraduates, though I'm as baffled as you as to why he's here."

"All in good time, Professor, Detective Inspector," said Ant.

Ant watched the colour drain from Pullman's face.

"This gentleman, Detective, likes to be in charge. In fact, he insists on everything being done his way. Isn't that so, Professor?"

Pullman uncrossed his arms and brushed imaginary mud from his trouser knees, trying hard to look in control.

"If you mean I insist on my staff being professional at all times, then I plead guilty." Pullman puffed out his chest and wafted a hand at Ant as if to bat away his accusation.

"Quite right, Professor," replied Ant before continuing. "You have a heavy responsibility that requires a firm hand. That's true, isn't it... Simon?"

The undergraduate froze at being singled out.

"Don't worry, Simon. I'm not asking you to criticise the professor. I know how important he is to your future. But all the same, he's not treated you well, has he?"

Simon gazed at the floor. Ant guessed he wished he was anywhere except in this tent.

Ant turned back towards the policeman.

"Did you know the professor is a whisky drinker, Detective Inspector?"

Ant could see Pullman was showing signs of panic.

"Look here. I had nothing to do with that nasty man's death. I—"

Ant interrupted.

"How did you know he was a nasty man, Professor? After all, it's not as if you're a local, is it?"

Ant could see the detective's eyes darting between the professor and him, unsure where the conversation was going. He guessed Riley was kicking himself for not checking the academic's drinking habit during his investigation of Narky's death.

"You may think we academics live in ivory towers," replied the professor, "but we see; we hear. I observed him in the pub and the way he treated people."

"Then you had a reason to dislike him?" said Ant.

Pullman glared at his interrogator, at one point rising from his chair, before thinking better of the idea.

"Don't be ridiculous, man. How might dislike morph into murder? And what about motive?"

Ant smiled. He had achieved his purpose.

"As you say, Professor. What motive might you have had?"

The academic settled back into his chair, unsure whether his interrogation had concluded or merely been paused.

"And talking about motive," said Ant as he turned towards Glen Dawson.

The carpenter froze at the unwanted attention.

"But Ant, I thought you believed me when I explained—"

Ant held an open palm towards Glen.

"The thing is, Glen, when we last met, you told me you hadn't seen Narky in the week leading up to his death. Isn't that so?"

Ant watched as the carpenter looked towards the tent entrance.

"No help out there, Glen."

Ant moved to his left, blocking any attempt the carpenter might make to bolt.

After a few seconds of silence, Glen responded.

"I admit it..."

Ant watched as Riley fumbled in his jacket.

Going for the handcuffs already, thought Ant.

"I confronted the nasty bugger in the Hall's stable block. I told him I'd had enough, and he could bugger off. I said I was going to shop him to you for fiddling all those invoices."

Ant closed the space between the carpenter and himself, looking down at the hapless man.

"But why didn't you tell me that before, Glen? Don't you trust me?"

He watched as Glen began to break down. It wasn't a sight he liked to watch.

"I was ashamed and thought you might think I'd done him in if you knew we'd been arguing. The day before he died, Narky got in such a rage, screaming and shouting. I thought he was going to clobber me. I think I might have threatened him. I can't remember, but I was scared. I ran out of the yard, and that's the last time I saw him, swear to God."

Ant allowed the carpenter to compose himself before addressing Riley.

"Detective Inspector, did you know Narky Collins was blackmailing Glen, and who knows how many other men in the village? One for the ladies was Narky, whether they wanted the attention or not."

Inspector Riley adopted his now all too familiar bemused look.

“The reason for the blackmail isn’t important, but—”

"But perhaps, a motive for murder," shot back Riley, gaining confidence he could take things from here.

"Mr Dawson, where were you on—"

"No, no," said Ant, cutting across the detective. "Glen didn't kill Narky Collins. I invited him here today only to show you just what a bad lot Narky was. Glen, like a few other men in the village were, I suspect, not too upset to hear of the man's death. But did he murder him? No."

Ant smiled at Glen, who he noticed was fidgeting with a toggle on his coat.

"Ant, I don't know whether to laugh or throw up. Are you telling me you believe me after all?"

Riley began to stand up, handcuffs in hand.

"Not so fast, Detective."

He turned back to Glen.

"Yes, I do believe you. As luck would have it, someone witnessed that argument."

Ant watched as Glen once more began to get tearful.

"I asked estate staff, who normally come across you, if they'd seen you with Narky. As it turns out, Graham, the stable lad, heard a kerfuffle as he was cleaning out my father's mare. I have to tell you it didn't look good for you... until he said he'd also seen you the next evening going into your workshop at the back of the stable block. He added you were making a hell of a din with your machines, by the way. So you see, if you'd told me when I first mentioned Narky to you, I could have checked your alibi out and informed the good detective here. As it is, you're lucky I asked around, aren't you?"

Ant approached Glen again, this time patting him on the shoulder as he watched the man visibly slump into his chair.

Riley sat down again, pushed the handcuffs back into his

pocket. It looked to Ant as if he were watching a man losing his bet on what he thought was a sure thing.

"I will check to see if your alibi stands up or if this is a fairy tale. Do you understand, Mr Dawson?"

The carpenter nodded. Ant could see he was exhausted by events.

"However, Detective Inspector, someone in this tent *did* commit a violent act the night Narky died."

Ant turned towards Vikki.

"Isn't that so, Miss King?"

The woman frowned as Ant turned towards her.

"A person who kept the fact secret, and which might have condemned her, until Lyn and I dragged the truth out of her."

All eyes fell on the detectorist.

Ant watched as her anger grew.

"But... but, I told you, I... You've been so kind. Why are you—?"

"Please do not confuse a single act of kindness with belief in your story, Miss King."

Ant could see he was unsettling the woman as she shifted nervously in her chair.

"And what have you to say about Miss King, Detective?"

Ant turned to the policeman, urging him to respond.

"But we interviewed dozens of them at the rally."

That one hit home, thought Ant, as he watched the detective do up then undo the buttons of his jacket.

"That may be so, but this lady hit a man that night and brought him to his knees. Isn't that correct, Vikki?"

She panicked and tried to run for it. Riley reacted in an instant and grabbed the terrified woman, restraining her arms while retrieving a pair of handcuffs from his jacket pocket for the second time.

"Vikki King," the inspector began, as he clamped the hard iron restraints on the woman's wrists. "Can you explain—"

"That won't be necessary," said Ant, cutting across the detective.

Ant knew he had again succeeded in angering Riley as he watched the detective's frustration bubble to the surface.

"Although Vikki did, indeed, clobber someone that night, it was self-defence. Isn't that right... Simon?"

Ant had managed, in one sentence, to confuse everyone in the tent. A brief silence was broken by the sound of Vikki gently crying, her eyes glistening with tears.

"Please, Detective, allow the young lady to resume her seat. She is not our murderer, as I shall explain in due course."

Ant touched a hand to his chin and looked at the floor.

"Now, what was I saying. Yes, that's it: Simon, you attacked Vikki, didn't you?"

The undergraduate failed to react to the resumption of Ant's interrogation. Instead, he concentrated on fiddling with his iPhone.

"Isn't that right, Simon."

This time Ant raised his voice, simultaneously wrestling the gadget from the young man's vice-like grip.

Simon avoided Ant's eyeline for several seconds.

"Specifically, Detective Inspector, this young man attacked Miss King last Friday night. Correct, Simon?"

He's a cool one, thought Ant as he watched the young man stare at Vikki then Detective Inspector Riley as if dumbfounded as to why anyone might accuse him of such a thing.

"Did you attack this lady, Mr Hangmead?" asked Riley as he released Vikki from the wrist restraints.

Ant broke off from Simon and searched the caller list of the undergraduate's mobile.

"Please don't do that. It's private."

Ant ignored the young man. He scrolled down the screen, stopping at one particular entry. He smiled as his thumb rested on the name he had been searching for.

"Leave it!" shouted Simon. His demand startling everyone, except Ant.

"It's him," said Vikki, her tone strong, angry, resolute.

This time the inspector's job involved restraining Vikki from lunging at the undergraduate.

Simon stood between attacker and target.

Relative calm restored, Ant handed the mobile to Lyn and resumed his interrogation.

"Do you have a receding-hair problem, Simon? I know a lot of men can be self-conscious about such things."

He watched as the young man first glare then smile dismissively and shake his head.

"Then why are you so wedded to your hat? Every time I've seen you, you've been wearing it. Even when it's dull. In fact, there's a distinct lack of sun in here, and yet there it sits upon your head."

Simon raised a hand and adjusted the visor as if checking it was still in place.

"Never give it a thought. It's just something I always wear. What's wrong with that?" he said, his voice giving away his growing nervousness.

"Oh, nothing," responded Ant casually. "It's the neck cover that intrigues me. I'm sure you'd feel better without it in this stuffy tent. Why not take the hat off? Here, let me help you."

As Ant neared, Simon stiffened.

"No, don't."

Ant reached forward to lift the hat from Simon's head.

"There we go. Now, isn't that better?"

The undergraduate placed a hand over the back of his neck.

"What do we have here, my friend?"

Simon bristled. His nostrils flared.

"Let's show these good people what you've been hiding," said Ant as he spun Simon 180 degrees.

The manoeuvre exposed a two-inch gash, red raw with a flap of scabbed skin covering the injury.

"Bloody hell," said Vikki. "It was you who jumped me. That's where I hit you with my detector. Git, you could have killed me."

Simon struggled against Ant's firm hold.

"More like you could have killed me. I thought you were a nighthawk stealing from the dig site. All I was doing was protecting our work, that's all," replied Simon.

Ant watched the professor smile at his undergraduate, proud that a member of his staff had proved his loyalty to the team.

His indulgence didn't last long.

"Oh, if only that were true," said Ant, his grip tightening as Simon struggled. "Vikki was nowhere near the dig area, at least not the official one. But she *was* close to an area you wanted for yourself. You didn't know she'd left her detector after fending you off, only to come back later to retrieve it. It was then she saw a tall, thin man standing over a fat bloke. Also, she's just identified you as the man she heard shouting 'Leave it down there.'"

Simon ceased his struggle as he attempted to gather his thoughts.

"But she couldn't have seen me later. I was with my girl-friend. I can prove it. How could I be in two places at once?"

Across the tent, Lyn flicked the screen of the undergraduate's mobile phone before glancing in Ant's direction. She offered an almost imperceptible nod of her head.

Good, you've seen that name too, thought Ant.

"You can come in now, Tina."

Ant spoke just loud enough to penetrate the tent's canvas structure.

Lyn's school secretary entered, followed by a young woman. Ant watched Lyn smile at Tina, acknowledging a job well done.

"This, Detective Inspector, is Wendy Jones. She is also one of the professor's undergraduates... and sometimes girlfriend of Mr Hangmead. Isn't that right, Simon?"

Simon threw Wendy a menacing look. She turned away.

"Simon is right in one sense. He *should* have been with this young lady. But he didn't show up, did he, Wendy?"

Simon attempted to intervene.

"Wendy... tell them..."

The young woman concentrated her eyes on Riley.

"We should have met, but he didn't show. The next day he told me the professor had called an urgent meeting he had to attend. Stupidly, I believed him."

Professor Pullman shook his head as Riley looked at the academic for confirmation.

"I later checked with a few of the other undergraduates. There was no meeting. I thought he was cheating on me like he has before, so when Lyn came across me that night I... I...'

Ant took the opportunity to focus their attention back on the angry, young man.

"So what happened, Simon?" asked Ant in a quiet but determined tone that required an answer.

Simon looked around before sitting down and casually crossing his legs and his arms.

"I don't know what you're talking about. I've done nothing wrong except stand up my girlfriend for—"

"For what, Simon?"

Ant cut across the undergraduate hoping to throw him off guard.

"A village girl I met weeks ago. Very obliging, you know, these locals."

Lyn caught Ant's attention.

"May I have a word with Casanova, here?"

Ant held an arm out towards the young man.

"I thought you might." He smiled as Lyn stepped forward.

"Two-timing a girlfriend is never a good idea, chappie. It always comes back to bite you. But for the sake of our general amusement, let's play your little game, shall we?"

Ant was intrigued where Lyn was about to take things.

"Of course, you know I am the local head teacher, don't you? That means all the local children go through my hands at some point in their lives. Not only that, but I like to keep tabs on my charges as they grow, and as you say, this is a small place. So do tell me the name of your latest conquest, Simon?"

Ant watched the undergraduate's smile fade as he narrowed his eyes. It was the same look he'd seen the young man give the professor when being told off for questioning the importance of a find he had dropped. This time Ant could see the man was having trouble controlling his anger.

Better get ready to get between these two, he thought.

"I can't remember," replied Simon, brushing Lyn's question aside with disdain.

Better be careful, young fella. She's onto you, thought Ant.

"Really? You'll have to do better than that for the detective, here."

Ant flicked a glance at the policeman. He appeared pleased to have been acknowledged.

"Felicity. Her name was Felicity—"

"Do we have such a lady in the village, Lyn?" interrupted Ant.

He watched as his friend's face lit up like a candle.

"Ah yes, I know Felicity. Such an unusual name, Simon. In fact, we have just one Felicity in the village."

Ant turned his attention back to the undergraduate. He was clutching the sides of his seat so hard his knuckles had turned white.

"Now unless our Felicity, or Flo as we know her, has turned into a cougar, she wouldn't be your type, Simon."

Ant was joined in a throaty giggle by Glen.

"You see, Flow is a ninety-three-year-old."

The laughter increased with Ant leading the chorus.

"Now you've got me intrigued, Simon. Do tell us more."

The undergraduate's shoulders slumped for a moment. It wasn't long before he regained his composure.

"So, her name wasn't Flo... or whatever. It was..."

"Stop it. Stop it now, and tell the truth. Just for once."

Ant, like everyone else, including Simon, was startled by Wendy's anguished intervention.

The occupants of the tent fell into complete silence. Ant watched as Wendy's eyes burned into Simon's expressionless face.

"Let's drop the charade, Simon. There was no other girl. There was no urgent meeting with the professor. You were too busy doing more important things as you saw it. Is that not the case?"

Ant studied his foe's body language closely as he spoke.

"I've only met you a few times, and fleetingly at that, and yet I watched as your anger almost got the better of you. Now let's say you had a deal with Narky, and he tried to double-cross you. Perhaps on that particular night you couldn't hold your temper and hit out. It might even have been self-defence. But either way, your actions resulted in that man's death. Isn't that so?"

Ant half expected Simon to erupt and allow his bubbling anger free reign. Instead, the undergraduate's demeanour slowly, imperceptibly at first, began to change. As he relaxed back into his chair he began to smirk.

"He got greedy. Stupid, ignorant thugs always do." I found a hoard of gold coins. All my own research. It took months of trawling through archives. The professor thinks I'm stupid. Well, look who found the gold."

Professor Pullman blinked as he took in the enormity of Simon's confession and the consequences for his professional reputation.

"Anyway, that stupid fool somehow found out. Don't ask me how. He came sniffing around and said he would tell the professor if I didn't give him a cut of the money."

Ant put his hands into his pockets and spoke in a calm, measured voice.

"So, you murdered him?"

Simon glanced at Ant who watched as his smirk broadened into a smile, shrugged his shoulders, and swung his crossed leg up and down as if maintaining the beat of a favourite music track.

"I told you, he got greedy. I agreed to pay him to keep him quiet, but then I came across him excavating the hoard. He must have been watching me for days. Anyway, he got what he deserved. His fault, not mine. Simples."

Ant could see the casualness of Simon Hangmead's

confession appalled everyone, except him and Riley. They'd listened to such excuses for murder many times.

"So you killed him and staged the scene?" said the detective inspector.

Simon laughed.

"He took some getting into that trench, the fat sod. But yes, I found a piece of a detector and couldn't believe my luck when I saw her initials on it. Then I found that note from him." Simon pointed to Glen. "I stuck it in the dead bloke's hand and closed his fist around it then put the stone under his head. Job done. Oh, except for the whisky. I think that was a great touch, don't you?"

Even Ant now flinched at the cold-heartedness with which the young man spoke.

"Except, Simon," said Ant, "Narky Collins didn't drink whisky. If you had used beer, you might have got away with it, except you aren't as clever as you think, are you?"

The undergraduate's smile vanished.

The tent fell silent, except for the quiet weeping of Wendy as she realised her gentle, well-mannered boyfriend was, in reality, a callous murderer.

EPILOGUE

"Lord Stanton," said Detective Inspector Riley as he slipped into the passenger seat of the police Jaguar. "You were right about Simon hiding the hoard in that spoil heap. However, next time I'll arrest you for obstruction and concealing evidence. Do we understand one another?"

Ant raised his right hand to his forehead as if doffing an imaginary cap.

Riley turned to glare at Ant as the police car sped from Stanton Hall in a cloud of dust.

"Let me guess," said Lyn as she linked arms and strolled into the walled garden with her best friend. "I'm thinking he wasn't inviting you to the station Christmas party this year?"

"Er, no. But I got a 'thank you.' At least that's how I take not getting myself arrested, anyway. And another thing—would you believe he almost got my title right!"

Ant felt the gentle squeeze of Lyn's hand on his arm. Both laughed.

"So our dear detective inspector knows you're a real lord!"

"It would seem so, Lyn."

There followed a cry of pain as Ant reacted to Lyn pinching the soft flesh of his exposed arm.

"What was that for?"

"To prick that pompous ego of yours."

"Joking. I was joking."

Ant attempted to massage out the pain and offered Lyn sight of his injury.

Lyn giggled.

"All the same, you need reminding."

Ten minutes passed as the pair strolled along the meandering gravel path of the enclosed garden. From time to time, one or the other would extend a hand to catch the top of a rose or line of lavender. They reached the bench they'd last sat on one week earlier.

"So what will you do?" asked Lyn, her tone serious.

Ant knew what Lyn meant. He hesitated. Instead, he tracked a flock of geese as they flew over the great house.

As the seconds ticked away, he knew Lyn expected an answer.

"I report to my commanding officer on Monday morning. After that, a medical assessment. Then we'll see."

Lyn swayed to her left and gently body bumped Ant. It was her way of letting him know she understood.

"The thing is, Lyn, whether they pass me fit or not, there's Mum and Dad to think about, let alone this place."

Lyn turned to look at her friend.

"Sounds as if you've made up your mind?"

Ant returned her look before cricking his neck to catch the last of the geese disappear.

"Perhaps you're right. If you think about it, who needs a battlefield with murders to solve around here?"

"I'll tell you what," said Lyn. "You solve the murders and fix the Hall's roof, and I'll keep the chocolate cakes coming for your mum and dad and do my Dr Watson act on you. Deal?"

Ant smiled.

"Are you asking, or telling?"

END

GLOSSERY

UK English to American English

- **Bap:** Bread roll
- **Bobbie:** Cop
- **Broad:** A stretch of water formed from old peat diggings. Common in Norfolk and Suffolk regions of the UK. Can take the form of narrow stretches of water like canals, or open water like small lakes.
- **Buttercross:** Medieval term used to describe a standing cross, or open-sided small building, where foodstuffs and other goods were exchanged, usually in villages or small towns.
- **Car bonnet:** Hood
- **Car boot** Trunk
- **Collard:** Slang word for catching or getting hold of or catching a person. Sometimes used in context of the police; "He was collard and taken to the police station. Also e.g. "My friend collard me and talked for ages".

- **Cottage pie:** Traditional dish cooked in a dish comprising a beef base (mincemeat) and mashed potato topping. Can include carrots, onion, celery and other vegetables to hand.
- **'Daft as a brush':** Friendly admonishment for being behaving in a silly way.
- **Gobbledygook:** Something that doesn't make sense. "You're talking gobbledygook, Jim." Normally used in a friendly, informal manner, rather than as an insult.
- **Jezza:** Short-form 'slang' for male first name 'James'.
- **Jiffy bag:** A padded bag used for shipping fragile contents.
- **Long-case clock:** Grandfather clock, for example
- **Meths:** short form for methylated spirit
- **Mobile phone:** Cell phone
- **Oiks:** Rude or unpleasant person. Sometimes used lightheartedly, e.g. "Hey, behave, you little oik."
- **Plod:** nick-name for a policeman or "the police"
- **Primary school:** Elementary school
- **Public school:** A school were all fees are paid by the student's parents/guardians (as opposed to a state school, which is free).
- **Straw boater:** A traditional flat-topped hat with a wide brim and decorative ribbon. Now mainly used by people attending sailing regattas.
- **Tenner:** Colloquial term for a ten-pound note (UK currency)
- **The Big House:** Often used by village residents to describe the local manor house. In Scotland

the term is sometimes used to describe a local prison.

- **Tied Cottage:** An old fashioned landlord/leaseholder arrangement not often used now but historically common in farming and mining. The landowner built the house (often of poor quality), rented it to his employee, but when the farmworker or miner left their employment, the family would HAVE to move out of the cottage.
- ***Time Team*:** A popular UK TV show that sets a team of archaeologists the challenge of digging and interpreting an historical site or feature over three days.
- **Toff:** Slang word for upper-class or rich person generally seen to be "looking down" on other people.
- **Wallop:** To hit someone, 'I gave him a good wallop'.
- **Wellies or Wellingtons:** Rain Boots. Footwear that extend to just below the knee. Usually used for walking or country sports in poor weather. Said to have been named after the Duke of Wellington.
- **Wherry:** A traditional sailboat used for carrying goods and passengers on the Norfolk & Suffolk Broads

JOIN MY READERS' CLUB

Getting to know my readers is the thing I like most about writing. From time to time I publish a newsletter with details on my new releases, special offers, and other bits of news relating to the Norfolk Murder Mystery series. If you join my Readers' Club, I'll send you this gripping short story free and ONLY available to club members:

A Record of Deceit: 17,000 word short story

Grace Pinfold is terrified a stranger wants to kill her. Disturbing phone calls and mysterious letters confirm the threat is real. Then Grace disappears. Ant and Lyn fear they have less than forty-eight hours to find Grace before tragedy strikes - a situation made worse by a disinterested Detective Inspector Riley who's convinced an innocent explanation exists.

Character Backgrounds: A 7,000 word insight

Read fascinating interviews with the four lead characters in the Norfolk Cozy Mysteries series. Anthony Stanton, Lyn Blackthorn, Detective Inspector Riley and Fitch explain what drives them, their backgrounds and let slip an insight into each of their characters. We also learn how Ant, Lyn and Fitch first met as children and grew up to be firm friends - even if they do drive each other crazy most of the time!

You can get your free content by visiting my website at www.keithjfinney.com

I look forward to seeing you there.

Keith

AFTERWORD

Did you enjoy Dead Man's Trench?

Reviews are so important in helping get my books noticed. Unlike the big, established authors and publishers, I don't have the resources available for big marketing campaigns and expensive book launches (though I live in hope!)

What I *do* have is the following of a loyal and growing band of readers.

Genuine reviews of my writing help bring my books to the attention of new readers.

If you enjoyed this book, it would be a great help if you could spare a couple of minutes and head over to my Amazon or Goodreads author page to leave a review (as short or long as you like).

Thank you so much.

For Joan, A Very Special Lady.

ACKNOWLEDGMENTS

Cover design by Books Covered

Edit & Proofreading: Paula.
paulaproofreader.wixsite.com/home

PUBLISHED BY:
Norfolk Cozy Mystery Publishing

keith@keithjfinney.com
facebook.com/keithjfinneyauthor

WWW.KEITHJFINNEY.COM

ALSO BY KEITH FINNEY

In the Norfolk Murder Mystery Series:

Murder by Hanging

Ethan Baldwin, a respected resident of Stanton Parva, hangs from a tree in Woods on the edge of the village. Detective Inspector Riley is convinced he committed suicide. Ant and Lyn are sure he's been murdered. But who would want to kill the church warden? They set out to find justice for Ethan, but will Riley stop them in their tracks?

The Boathouse Killer

Geoff Singleton was wealthy, successful, and hadn't a care in the world having recently married the love of his life, Hanna.

Except someone murdered him.

A jealous boyfriend from Hanna's past is seen in the village.

An investor in the victim's investment company stands to lose a fortune.

Fake police officers throw their weight around.

Yet Detective Inspector Riley refuses to believe anything untoward has happened. Emotions run high as Ant and Lyn work to find Geoff's killer... before they can strike again.

www.keithjfinney.com

Facebook

Printed in Great Britain
by Amazon

46241390R00092